voices from the
Blue Hotel

fictions

by

maya sonenberg

D1527687

chiasmus press
PORTLAND

Chiasmus Press

www.chiasmuspress.com
press@chiasmusmedia.net

PRODUCED AND PRINTED IN THE UNITED STATES OF AMERICA
ISBN: 0-9785499-4-5

cover design: Lidia Yuknavitch
cover photo: Seneca Ray Stoddard, 1889
layout design: Matthew Warren
author photo: Wendy Madar

Acknowledgements

Grateful acknowledgement is made to the editors of the following magazines in which these stories first appeared, sometimes in slightly different form: *Alaska Quarterly Review*: "Shadow Play"; *American Fiction, Volume Ten: The Best Unpublished Stories by Emerging Writers*: "Beyond Mecca"; *American Short Fiction*: "This Thing About Boys"; *Caffeine Destiny*: "The House Had Many Rooms"; *Gargoyle, 20th Anniversary Issue*: "Baby 1995"; *Gulf Stream*: "Noctambus"; *Other Voices*: "Memento Mori"; *Passages North*: "Proximity to the Body of the Star"; *Princeton Arts Review*: "Throwing Voices"; *Santa Monica Review*: "Wanting What We Don't Want."

"Beyond Mecca" also appeared in *Birds in the Hand: Fiction and Poetry about Birds* (ed. Dylan Nelson and Kent Nelson; North Point Press: New York, 2004).

"The House Had Many Rooms" also appeared in *Northwest Edge 3: The End of Reality* (ed. Andy Mingo, Trevor Dodge, Lidia Yuknavitch; Chiasmus Press: Portland, OR, 2006).

Thanks to Hal Hartley and Impossible Films for permission to quote from the film *Simple Men*. Copyright © 1992, 2002 by Hal Hartley.

IN MEMORY OF MY MOTHER

PHOEBE HELMAN SONENBERG, 1926-1994

Table of Contents

There is no such thing as adventure. There's no such thing as romance. There's only trouble and desire.

—*Simple Men*, Hal Hartley

THE HOUSE HAD MANY ROOMS

IT WASN'T THE DROUGHT that summer—three months without rain so that cars driving up the hill billowed huge clouds of dust that settled again on the black locust trees in the yard and also on the Persian carpet in the living room which meant we had to vacuum every day. It wasn't the heat—ten days in a row with temperatures above 90 (very unusual for this part of the country). It wasn't the damp that crept through every crack, made all the curtains go limp, and straightened out the curls Mother twisted into our hair. It wasn't the spiders in the linen closet or the mosquitoes hovering around the mudroom sink. It wasn't the mice that scurried through the garage during the day and scampered through all the bedrooms at night, hiding caches of birdseed in dresser drawers, rocking chair cushions, and laundry baskets for the winter. It wasn't the locusts that swarmed the vegetable garden and took up residence in the gazebo, the wasps building a nest under the eaves just outside our playroom, the ants marching ceaselessly along the counter in the bathroom and circling the faucet, or the lone cricket trapped behind the refrigerator whose chirps echoed off the tin ceiling and kept us awake until we went downstairs and flushed it out with a broom, bringing with it an old soap dish and several dead moths and also the plug that we forgot to plug back in while we inspected the cricket, and all the food, all the butter and milk and eggs and leftover chocolate pudding, spoiled so that we could only have dry toast and tea for breakfast. It wasn't the Madagascar jasmine plant in the dining room, which sent out its long tendrils every which way, searching for something to twine around, even our necks if we sat too close. And it wasn't the strange smell of old sweat that came from the lamp in our parents' room. It wasn't even the fact that the hurricane lifted the roof off the conservatory and then set it down again with a crash in a far corner of the garden, the whole glass roof in smithereens. After the hurricane passed, the wind shifted to the northwest and brought two days of smoke and ash from forest fires in Quebec. One million acres burned and we had a day without a real dawn. All the birds were silent and every one in town called the fire chief to find out if their neighbor's house over the ridge had burnt to the ground, but it wasn't any of these plagues that led to our ruin, although they were bad enough (we were only waiting for frogs). And it wasn't even that both of the cats came home one morning dragging broken legs or that Archie the Dog kept chewing himself raw, that the budgie had pneumonia (have you ever heard a bird wheeze and cough?) or that sometimes when we surprised him, Father seemed unable to speak.

It wasn't the music pounding through the pine forest and over the blueberry fields late at night as if somebody had misplaced it, a heavy drum and screeching guitars and someone screaming. It came from the Sugar Shack, the only bar in town, where the fat bouncer in the striped shirt asked every girl who walked up to the door to marry him (even us!); where the red and black floor tiles were so dirty our bare feet stuck to them when we wandered in there during the day; where bands from the city played to five or six unfriendly summer kids. At night we snuck out our bedroom window, shinnied down the drainpipe, and traipsed over there. We stood in the gravel parking lot in our thin summer nightgowns and watched the flickering neon sign and listened. Sometimes we put broken pieces of beer bottles in front of all the tires in the parking lot, and on the way back home sometimes we could find porcupines squished on the road. It also wasn't the weirdness of having another sort of music, Mozart and Brahms Mother said, waft down the road from the other direction where the violin and cello and piano students practiced from dawn to noon and then again from four to seven. In between, they had lunch and a swim. We knew this because sometimes one of them baby-sat for us. We made her sit in the middle of the porch swing, the one with flowered cushions, while we sat on either side and asked questions like what was it like to kiss a boy and could she feel anything with all those calluses on her fingertips. When she stopped answering, we played with her long brown hair until it was

2

time for bed, braiding it, teasing it, curling it around orange juice cans just like in the illustrations we'd cut out of magazines Mother had been saving for the recipes.

It wasn't any of these things, not even that at the end of the day when Mother called us in, we looked up at the big house, at the gables and balconies and attic dormers, at the shingles that kept falling from the north turret, and thought all the windows were blinking at us in a Morse Code we couldn't decipher. We decided to bring in the pies we'd made out of mud from the toxic waste dump. They smelled wicked, but we still tried to pass them off as dessert. Even so, we felt like amoebas or paramecia or one of those other tiny protozoa things you can only see under the microscope—except when we did something wrong or there was some chore for us to do: water the geraniums or feed the fish but not too much. (It was always too much; no matter how little we fed them, the fish kept dying.)

No, it was that, when we wandered up and down the halls during siesta time or early in the morning before our parents were awake, we heard a different human sound coming from each room: moaning, wailing, laughing, screaming, chattering, singing, chewing.... and we knew that, in the last room, safe from all those noises behind a locked door, Mother and Father were whispering, they were making plans to escape.

We watched them every second, Mother and Father, focused completely on their plans—because we knew something was going on. They would say it was a lie, that they were paying attention to us too, but we knew better. We knew they were deciding which relatives to give the house to, with us and the furniture included. We watched the way their hands intersected while passing a salt shaker, then sprang apart again like tricky magnets. We watched the way Mother's eyes followed Father and Father's eyes followed Mother, just as if all those eyes had their own legs and feet. We became trackers too, our noses sharp as Archie the Dog's nose, sharp to the scent of yells or kisses. Did you know that kisses have a smell? But like Archie with rabbits, we never caught up to them. We heard the hesitation when Mother asked Father or Father asked Mother, just before dinner, how the day had been and what they'd been doing at lunch time that kept them from the table. "Oh, you know, Fourth of July," he said. "I was in town buying Catherine Wheels and Sparklers for the children.

3

Randy works for that company over in Blue Hill and he was
telling me what a pain it is to make those things, even the
little ones." Or she said, "The children....," even though she
hadn't been anywhere near us at lunch time. Even though
we'd eaten our peanut butter and pickle sandwiches alone
while they wandered separately in and out of the house, and
we never saw if Mother or Father had any lunch at all. From
all these things, we <u>knew</u> something was going on. They
should have been paying attention to <u>us</u>, talking to <u>us</u>, playing
with <u>us</u>. We still get mad when we think how we promised
not to eat the last of the strawberries for them, how we gave
up biting our nails, and picked up all the toys from the front
walk, even the bicycle and the skateboard (which isn't much
good on the dirt road anyway) and the plastic Mr. Potato Head
who really preferred to stay outside. After all that, they were
<u>still</u> always looking somewhere else, and we knew because
we watched them.

They say it's because we were jealous but that's not true. When
we were younger, we did get jealous, elbowing each other
out of the way or pulling each other's hair, but not anymore.
"You little green-eyed monsters," Mother called us, laughing,
when we followed her around (and we <u>do</u> have green eyes,
all of us), like that day we went with her into town and she
stopped right next to Bill Hinshaw who owns the hardware
store and talked about the price of nails, the best way to kill
roaches, and the history of fireworks book we'd made her read
to us on the lawn in front of the library, until we each fished a
quarter out of her purse and swallowed it to get her attention.
After Bill Hinshaw turned us upside down and whacked us
on the back until the quarters popped out again, she yelled at
us, but then she crouched down and smoothed our hair out of
our faces. We thought of swallowing coins again and again
just so she would do that—kneel down and look straight into
our eyes and touch our faces with her smooth hands. "Don't
tell your father," she said. "He'll be furious." But he didn't
pay much attention to us either. Late at night (it was late for
<u>us</u>), we'd creep downstairs and find Father in the little room
off the kitchen. He'd have a calculator and papers spread all
over the table, but he'd be holding a big book in his hands
and not reading it. Instead he seemed to be staring at the
ceiling and listening for something or sometimes he'd be

4

talking on the phone and he'd hang up as soon as he saw us. He'd say, "Quit staring. Go back to bed." But we demanded that he take us outside and tell us our favorite story about the stars all over again—how they were balls of fire that God set spinning like yo-yos on a string, and the constellations were what happened when all the strings got tangled—while the bats flitted and darted between us. We wanted to tire him out and to distract him from plotting what to do with us, but finally we'd succumb to tiredness ourselves and agree to go back to bed. On the way upstairs, we stopped to see if salamanders had invaded the refrigerator or lobsters and crabs were sleeping in the toilet tank, and we could hear Father return to his phone conversation, talking softly so we couldn't tell what he was saying. Then in the long upstairs hall, we stopped again and put our ears to every door, we looked through every keyhole even though all we ever saw was a chair leg or the corner of a bed or some discarded piece of clothing (a pair of pants in one room, a brassiere in another), because we thought we heard Mother's voice in every room, just as if she were on the other end of the phone, talking to Father. We hoped and hoped she was, even though we knew she wasn't—that was silly—and they never talked to each other anymore except when they had to.

    They say it's because we were jealous but we weren't jealous, and we don't know where the flames came from any better than anyone else. Mother and Father scooped us out of our beds and held us tight to their chests as they raced downstairs. We could feel them close, feel them breathing in our ears, smell their minty toothpaste. We weren't afraid and we thought that at least if the flames got us, we would all melt together. Then we stood outside in one tight little group (they held our hands and wouldn't let go) and watched each room blow up with a different color—red in the bedrooms, green in the dining room, indigo in the kitchen—just as if someone had sprinkled a different trace metal in with the perchlorate and sulfur and charcoal on each of the different floors before they lit the match—but who would do something like that? Who would know which metals would make which colors and how to make it all explode? That's what we want to know.

5

"UP IN THE SKY, THERE'S Orion, right over the Wilsons' house," my mother says. "Do you see him? It should be easy; it's so dark tonight. I'm pointing right at his head, that one tiny star. Do you see him now? Those are his shoulders—the stars placed far apart. And his legs. And his belt slung low on his hips—that's the thing to recognize him by."

It's a belt to hang weapons from, I think, but my mother's saying it's a rhinestone belt. She starts humming "Rhinestone Cowboy" and I'm just glad no one can hear her. I think six-shooter, sword, spear, and I can't remember why Orion got tossed up into the sky, what he did on earth to get turned into a constellation.

We're standing and shivering together out in the front yard, sharing a cigarette. She won't stop smoking but she doesn't want the smell in the house, even now that she's moving out, moving back East to be near her sisters. I'm home to help her pack. When I talked to her on the phone, she seemed frail to me, and I couldn't stand the thought of her lugging boxes around by herself. We moved into this house when I was ten, and I remember my father going out to get burgers and fries while we waited for the furniture to arrive. We ate our lunch sitting on the floor, right in the middle of the room. When we were done, my mother lay down and put her head on my father's thigh, and I lay down and put my head on his other thigh. She talked about where the couch should go and where to hang the paintings. I looked up at the white ceiling, contented.

Now we keep passing the cigarette back and forth, each taking a drag, the orange cinder floating between us in the dark. Every spring I quit for a while. Then I see a friend tap the filter end on a table, lean forward, stop talking as she lights it. She looks just like Lauren Bacall, and I just have to have one. I think I've had so many, one more won't kill me. But I don't smoke a lot, just one, once in a while. When my mother and I are done, when we've smoked it right down to the filter, she drops the butt on the walk and crushes it with her foot. I stand with my arms crossed over my chest, looking up at the stars. "Let's go in. You look cold," she says.

In the living room, there are candles burning everywhere, on the mantle and on every table. All the lamps are packed and we're burning every candle left in the house, every taper and every stub left from some ancient dinner party, every birthday candle stuck in a damp sponge since there's no cake and we're both on diets anyway. Their light is flickery and faint, but my mother says candlelight makes our eyes and cheeks glow. For whom? I wonder. Who's going to see us? She pours us each a drink, makes me sit on the couch next to her, and starts turning pages in an old photo album, the pictures all a faded brownish black. She tells me stories about them. Some I've heard before; some I think she's inventing right now.

"I met the boy in this picture before we could really speak English so we made up a language our parents couldn't understand." She's tapping a photo of two kids who look like they're about six years old. They're both wearing striped shirts and have short haircuts with bangs. They're grinning at each other wickedly, and I can't tell which is the boy and which is the girl. Neither of them looks anything like my mother. "I remember our fathers used to throw us up in the air and threaten not to catch us," she says and laughs. "His family had a cabin in the mountains, and I spent part of a summer there once when my sisters were in camp. All I remember is him telling me jokes I couldn't stop laughing at. I laughed so hard I couldn't breathe and my cheeks ached. Even then I knew they were stupid jokes but <u>he</u> was telling them.... I think I was scared he wouldn't like me because I couldn't make him laugh that way." She smiles brightly, drinks scotch from the glass she's holding, turns the page.

She seems brisker than I remember, businesslike and brittle. She's cut her hair very short, close to the skull, and has taken to wearing Nikes and leggings and too-large sweaters in bright colors. Tonight she's wearing a pink one that matches her lipstick and nail polish.

7

"Here's my second grade class, all lined up," she says. "The kids in the back row were standing on metal folding chairs. That's the teacher, Miss Newman. She had red hair and used to clap her hands together to get our attention. The girls were her favorites. See, she has her arms around the three of us— me, Karen, and Sarah. The rest of the kids were boys, twenty boys."

My mother and her friends are wearing pale dresses with fluffy skirts, and the twenty boys are all wearing ties and have their hair slicked back.

"This one was my second grade boyfriend, Ricky." She points to a boy with a missing tooth. "That tooth didn't fall out. It got knocked out when Angelo dared him to jump from the top bar of the jungle gym and he tripped when he hit the ground. I remember. At the end of the year, before he moved away, he gave me a tiny wooden tiger with tiny teeth and tiny painted stripes. I kept losing it, and each time I found it, more paint had chipped off. Your father was with me when I found it once. I said, 'Oh look at this,' and told him what it was. He got jealous. I could tell because he wouldn't talk to me for the rest of the afternoon, and later, he kept asking me which of his presents I was going to keep."

"That must have been years later. And he was still jealous?"

"It was funny, actually. I knew it meant I had him," she says. She gets up and starts rummaging in one of the boxes.

"Do you still have it?"

"I don't know." She straightens up and puts her hands on her hips. "Even if I do, I don't know where it would be." She walks around, brushing each pile of boxes with the palm of her hand. In the candlelight, they all look unstable.

The living room is full of stuff out of its usual place and so is the dining room and the kitchen and all the bedrooms, stuff waiting to be thrown out or packed up or given away. I'm taking this couch and some dishes, nothing else. In my old room, the posters of James Dean have finally been taken down and you can see pale rectangles on the walls where they used to be. Where he used to be, sitting with his boot crossed over his other knee, chewing on a straw or some such thing, holding a Stetson hat. In the afternoons after school, I'd sit on my bed and imagine I was in *Giant* where I'd save him from ever turning into that mean old drunk who falls off the dais at his own banquet. In *East of Eden*, I'd be the Julie Harris character but not so prissy. I'd ride the top of that train with him from Salinas to Monterey, from lettuce fields to the cool Pacific. I'd help him look for his mother and comfort him when he found out she was a whore. He'd kiss me shyly. I'd kiss him harder.... I wouldn't say I masturbated when I looked at those posters, but perhaps I did. Put a hand between your legs, and what is it anyway but the imagination lashed to the body. When I'd come to, I'd be surprised to find myself in the same old room with its dark blue curtains, three hundred miles from the ocean. Sometimes, now, I wake up in the middle of the night, find the dark has collapsed around me like sand in a sinkhole, and think I'm in that room. Or really in any room next to my parents' room, and that my father is asleep there, breathing evenly, untroubled. Once we walked through a cornfield together, the stalks much higher than my head. He picked an ear of corn for me to eat raw, stripping the husk and silk away, and the air had the wet, green, dirt smell of summer. During the day, I never think of him. It's only now, sitting here, that I can really imagine seeing him again. When I was little, he'd sit right at the edge of his chair, lean forward, and clasp his hands between his knees if the conversation interested him. Other times, he stared out the window, and soon he'd just get up and leave, even if you were right in the middle of saying something. Sometimes my mother would follow him from room to room for half an hour until he paid attention.

9

The next photo shows a boy and two girls sitting on the bench in front of an ice cream parlor. "Do you recognize us—me and my sister, your Aunt Martha?" my mother asks. The boy's squinting into the sun, and she and my aunt are sitting on either side of him, turning their heads so they can look into his eyes. My mother's wearing a headband with three plastic daisies on it. She looks about eight which means Martha must be about twelve. They each have a hand on one of his knees. They're all wearing shorts, and the sun glints off their hair.

"Who was he?" I ask. "You're both looking at him so adoringly."

"You know, I don't remember. I remember his knee was too big for my hand to hold," my mother says. "I don't remember what he was saying, but I remember watching

Martha's hand creep up his thigh toward the edge of his shorts until I slapped it. I must have been jealous. I followed him around that entire summer, and now I can't even remember his name." She laughs. "Look at him. You can see he was trying to impress someone, but it wasn't us. He isn't even looking at us. It must have been Annie. I bet she took this picture. She was about sixteen then and beautiful. She's still beautiful. I bet he was trying to impress her."

She turns the page and I take a long sip of my drink. She's mixed me a very strong rum and tonic, twisting lemon and lime into it.

"This is my father," she says, rubbing her finger over the face in the next picture. "You never knew him."

I want to say that I never met him but I know all about him. He was in the Coast Guard and he used to hit her. In the picture, he's wearing his white dress uniform and his eyes are closed as if he's asleep standing up. When I ask my mother, she insists that he wasn't. "I asked him," she says. "He always told me that he was just trying not to laugh because his brother was making faces at him from behind the camera. The call came when his eyes were still closed to go help with a shipwreck, some ship bringing war refugees from Germany. When he got there it was almost dark, the waves were tossing garbage against the sides of the cutter. They couldn't find anybody." She touches her cheek with her hand, and I see the new silver rings on each finger. The wedding band looks incongruous. She says, "Before he hit me, he always said, 'This is going to hurt me more than it hurts you.' Even then I knew it was a stupid thing to say, but when I heard the story behind this photo I began to understand."

I want her to turn the page. I'm tired of looking at her father.

"He hit hard, too," my mother says, "for a man who had to pull bodies from the water all the time."

The next one's a charmer. He's standing under a sycamore tree, smiling, sort of goofy, looking seductively into the camera. My mother sighs. "I was crazy about him. I thought he looked like Rock Hudson."

"He does," I say. He's got straight dark hair, long in the front, and I can imagine him whipping it out of his face with a snap of his head. I bet he wrote her silly notes in English class and used to throw pebbles against her window in the middle of the night when he had something he just had to tell her. I try to imagine my mother lusting after him when she was fifteen, standing next to him in a crowd while they watched the Fourth of July parade, letting their shoulders touch and then taking just one finger and stroking the inside of his arm where the tendon stands out—maybe his skin would be slightly sticky, damp with sweat—but I can't.

"He used to wear his baseball cap backwards with the bill sloping down his neck," she says. "I know. I know. All the boys wear them that way now but they didn't then. No one wore baseball caps at all then. Except he actually played baseball in high school so he had one. He was always smiling," she says. "Except for once when he turned his head aside in the middle of telling me something. We used to sit on his porch steps and talk for hours. This time he was telling stories about hunting with his uncles and having to eat bear meat and suddenly he just said, 'Well, I don't have to go into that,' and stared off into space for a while."

"What happened to him," I ask, "if you liked him so much?"

"Oh, he didn't like me the way I liked him. But he was very nice about it. He ended up moving to New York to be an actor and he'd write and say I could stay with him if I was ever in town. I called him once but by then he didn't remember me." She smiles. "Well, you really couldn't expect him to. It was years later."

Yes you could, I think, after you listened to all his stories, after he looked at you like this—his eyes in the photo sultry, smoldering. I try to think of all the guys I know now—lawyers and paralegals at work, guys I see every week on the stairmaster at the gym—and whether I'm crazy about any of them. While my mother goes to dump our drinks and get us fresh ones, I try to think if any boy's ever looked at me the way this charmer was looking at the camera when my mother took the picture. I can't think of any. I resist thinking that all the good ones are gone—that no guy looks at any girl that way anymore—because I know it's stupid, but I can't help remembering the first guy I slept with, back in high school. He had blond hair so soft I thought it would melt when I touched it and eyes the color of hard green olives. After school, he worked in a gourmet food store, and he always smelled of coffee and chocolate, but he wasn't sweet. The first time he

11

came in my mouth, it tasted like Clorox and I spit it out. He said, "Next time swallow it. Real women swallow it."

My mother sits down next to me again and we clink glasses. I joke about how she's trying to get through all the liquor in the house, afraid to transport it across state lines. "At the rate we go, though," I say, "we'll be here for about a year after the movers leave." We're drinking slowly but I'm starting to see things off-kilter, not really sure about distances or edges. I don't feel drunk but I know I'll stumble if a stand up.

She laughs with me and turns the pages of the album until she finds a picture of Aunt Annie all dressed up for a dance. Next to her, the boy looks stiff and serious. "Goodness. I was crazy about this boy too," she says. "He was Annie's boyfriend in college. I must have been twelve or thirteen, and she found me out. One day we were all at a picnic together and she said to me, 'I know it's impossible to eat when you're in love.' She kept looking at me while I was trying not to look at him, and I hated her. I wanted her to die."

"You said that to me once too," I say. My mother looks startled. "Remember when I was fourteen and I stopped eating? You asked if I was in love."

"Did I really say that? How stupid of me. I just remember worrying about you."

"I was in love," I say, "but I never would have told you about stuff like that."

"You still don't," she laughs.

"Actually, I saw him last summer, the first time in ten years. It was at a party. He'd broken his leg and he kept sending his wife to get him stuff to eat and drink from the buffet."

"Well, she must love him very much," my mother says. "It does happen, you know." She has that look on her face she gets when she watches old movies late at night. I agree with her even though I'm thinking how he turned out to be a real jerk. He kept ordering his wife around, thinking of something else she had to go get him so he could whisper to me. In my ear, his breath felt warm and damp, almost like a tongue. But when she finally came back with the last glass of white wine, she sat on the arm of his chair and brushed his hair off his forehead very tenderly. I think how I never once got to touch him and how his skin still looked like butterscotch.

"We should get back to packing," my mother says.

"It's late," I say. "Let's wait until tomorrow." I keep turning the pages of the photo album. There are no pictures of my father but that may just be because these were all taken before my mother met him. When I get to a picture of two boys standing with their arms around each other's shoulders, she puts her hand on my wrist to stop me.

"This one cried all the time," she says, pointing to the boy on the right, the one so nondescript he could be anyone. "That's right. That was Andy. I asked and asked but he could never tell me why. He was the first one I .... Well, you know."

I stare at her. I didn't know she'd ever slept with anyone before my father. I wonder if the evening's been building up to this moment when we share stories of our "first times" like college roommates, but she moves right on.

"And this was Bob, his best friend. He had a truck and we all used to go swimming together at the lake. If Andy started kissing me, Bob would get angry. He'd say, 'I'm going to leave and you're going to have to walk back to town.' He'd get so mad his cheeks would get flushed. Andy and I would just go off to the other end of the beach, and when we came back, Bob would be taking beer bottles out of a trash can and throwing them into the water so they didn't sink but floated down toward the garbage dump at the far end of the lake. In the sun, his hair was so fair it looked almost white. We knew he'd never just leave us there." She's smiling like she remembers a secret.

"So what happened to Andy?" I ask.

"Well, when we were seventeen, I thought I was going to marry him, but it just didn't work out. I decided he was a little bit dull. You know how it is."

I go into the kitchen to get us new drinks, holding both glasses in one hand so I can steady myself against the bookcase with the other. After the living room candlelight, it's bright in here. On all the counters, dishes are stacked neatly even though the movers are scheduled to pack these themselves. The wedding band china she actually got for her wedding, the set of Wedgwood she picked up at an auction, the set of twelve Italian dessert plates each painted with a different flower. My mother wants to make sure the movers don't miss anything, and right after dinner she suddenly felt compelled to find the creamer and sugar bowl set she needs to give me. The pieces are shaped like bunches of purple grapes and have vines forming the handles—really ugly.

13

While I crack the ice tray over the sink, I think about the idea that boys are dull, and I'm amazed my mother could decide that about the first guy she slept with, that she could decide it so casually. I feel a little bit like I've been sitting next to a foreign creature tonight, some wild bird with a hard beak that might make a racket if you so much as look at it wrong or then again might sing sweetly, one of those birds you wouldn't give your grandmother because you're afraid it could start to whistle or catcall. In college, I lived with a guy named Dave who had long red hair I liked to braid and a wide leather belt I'd grab onto when he started to walk too fast. He never ever said anything when we were alone together, but it took me two whole years to figure out he was boring, not me.

When I get back to the living room, my mother is lying with her head on one of the armrests and her feet up on the sofa cushions, something she never let me do when I was growing up. Her eyes are closed.

"I'm not asleep. Come sit down," she says.

I go and sit and pull her legs back onto my lap.

"Jennie, you're a sweetie to help with all this," she says. "And to put up with these stories about all my old boyfriends. I don't know what's gotten into me. I haven't looked at these pictures in years. It's like it happened to someone else."

"Well, there weren't that many boyfriends, Mom," I tease her and think of the boyfriends I've had whom I've never told her about. I wonder if I'll ever tell her about Christopher who made a bet with his best friend that he could get me into bed within a week of meeting me. He would have, too, but he didn't have any condoms, so we had to wait. Then he told me not to fall in love with him, and since all I could think about, all the time, was the way he cupped a match in his hand to light a cigarette so that it looked red like a fire in a cave and the way he squinted as he sucked in the smoke, since all I could think about was the way he stood while he smoked— weight on one leg, thumb hooked over his belt buckle and the other four fingers down the front of his pants—since every time I heard his voice outside my window I stopped breathing so I could hear it better, I figured that I probably shouldn't go to bed with him after all.

I wonder if I'll tell my mother or my daughter—if I ever have one—about Jerry who I went skiing with last winter or Mark who I met at the hotel where we stayed. One night he got very drunk on vodka and red wine and put on Jerry's hat. With his hard narrow face, it made him look like a cowboy. Then he took off all his other clothes and ran out into the snow before we could stop him. I stood on the steps and watched as he ran around just inside the floodlight's icy blue circle. He was holding his skinny arms out to the sides and making airplane noises, the breath coming out of his mouth like exhaust. I'd never seen him naked before even though we'd made love in a third floor bathroom with the frosted window half open and me backed up uncomfortably against the cold sink. I'd pulled him toward me tighter and tighter because I could barely feel him, as if my whole body had gone numb. There in the parking lot, when the light hit him, his chest looked porcelain as the inside of a cup. "Crash landing," he laughed and took a rolling dive into the snow, then lay there staring up at the sky. I tried to pull him up but he batted me away. Then he pulled me down into the snow next to him and stuck his hand up under my sweater. "I want to fuck you again," he said. "You're a really good fuck." Jerry was watching, but in the morning we all pretended nothing had happened. When we got back to the city, Jerry said, "I never want to see you again. How could you do that?" I said, "It's OK. I don't want to see you again either, either of you." And for a minute I felt my heart float up in my chest as if it had wings, as if it could lift me up so that I could fly around and do whatever I wanted and never have to explain anything to anybody.

15

At midnight, my mother and I go back outside for another cigarette. The air's even colder. Wisps of fog are rising from the damp grass but the sky's still clear. "Why have you been telling me about all these boys?" I ask.

"Well, why not?" she says. "They were sweet. I haven't thought about them in ages."

Sweet, I think. I think how boys' hearts are like small-fisted cherries—a teaspoon of juice for every tablespoon of stone. "What did your mother tell you about men?" I ask. She's looking off into the distance now, up at the sky.

"What did my mother tell us? She sat the three of us in a row and told us one day the right one would come along. When I asked her how I'd know it was the right one for me and not for one of my sisters, she said, 'You'll just know.' She wasn't every helpful but she was right. Three months after I met your father, I saw him walking down the street in the sun with his hand on another woman's shoulder. His head was tilted down toward hers, and I took a picture of them. Then when the picture was developed, she wasn't there. I was already pregnant with you, Sweetheart, though I didn't know it yet."

She stops talking and looks at me again, touches my hair very gently with the palm of her hand. I know this part of the story already, how my conception was a surprise but she's always been happy about it.

"When he found out, he came back to me and said he'd never look at another woman again, and he didn't—at least not when I could see."

I look at her and think how, despite all that, he's gone now. Kissing angels in heaven, my mother would say. How did she ever get so sentimental? She'd say that for him they all look like Brigitte Bardot. I look over at her, all shadowy and dark, and think how she looks absolutely nothing like Brigitte Bardot—not even when she laughs, not even with that bright lipstick.

16

I think about my friends, how we suddenly stop talking about movies we saw over the weekend, stop planning how we'll become partners in the firm and then kick all the old farts out, in order to whisper compliments—you're so beautiful today; you look like a diva. When one of us has a broken heart, the others gather round her, a phalanx. The heartbroken one, the one left behind, describes his eyes when he said goodbye, how they slid away and wouldn't look at her. She describes the color of his skin over his breastbone or the salty taste of it, and how once at the beach he circled her ankle completely with one of his hands, what his voice sounded like on the phone late at night when he wanted to come over but didn't want to have to ask. And we say, "It's because you're too smart. You're too beautiful. You scared him away," until she says she believes us. I want to believe that when one of us tells someone it's finally and really over, his friends gather round him the same way, but I just don't know.

I think how my father never hit me like my mother's father hit her, but how I used to find photos of other women in his wallet and wonder who they were. I think of the lovers I've had and the lovers my mother's had and how their images are dark, their outlines fuzzy. Sometimes I can only remember one thing about each man I've known, the one thing I desired, and if I think of it, it makes me desire him again. When the wind comes up, I shiver, delicious shaking, and for some reason I think of this guy I see every morning in the coffee shop. He always sits in a booth by the window and rests his chin on his hand while he reads the paper. He's a good head taller than me; I know because I made sure to go stand next to him at the cash register once. He smelled of Dove soap, wheat toast, and bacon, and a little of the mint he was putting in his mouth. I see the hard angle to his jaw and that his nose has been broken. I see how his shoulders stretch the cloth of his chambray shirt when he stands and tucks it in more tightly. I see where the hair's just been clipped away on the back of his neck, leaving a thin line of white skin next to the tan. It's all nothing special, I know, but still I see the way his short fingers grasp a knife and fork, and I imagine his hand brushing my cheek, my nerves so tender that I can feel the whorls of his fingertips on the skin just under my eyes. My mother goes in, but I stand out here in the cold because I don't want to let that feeling go. It makes me catch my breath and my heart skip a beat—those old clichés; it makes me think how men are different and distant, alluring and mysterious as the hum from power lines along a dark road when the stars scatter the sky just like this.

17

SHADOW PLAY

I'M DREAMING WHEN I first hear the phone ring, looking through the windows of a doll cottage and watching the rooms grow to human size. I stop in the doorway between living room and kitchen and look down at the bare linoleum. "Someone was murdered here," I think and see a stain spread at my feet like red lace. It's one of those dreams that should be terrifying but isn't, one of those dreams that make your friends shiver when you tell it to them even though you say you woke up smiling. In the dream Barry is gone, but I'm not scared, I'm not even lonely; instead, I start planning what I'll use to fill all the empty rooms since I have no furniture. I think of swing sets and tea tables, chaise longues, pots and pots of pink geraniums, and they appear magically, arranged just as I'd like. Then all the walls disappear, leaving forest and blue sky. Still the phone keeps ringing, the persistent ring of Kim's husband. He calls late at night now that he's taken off for Indonesia and my sister is staying with us. Dashing Paul and beautiful Kim. If he wants to talk to Kim, he'll never let up, so I push the quilts aside and ignore Barry's grumbling. He came home at ten like he has every night for at least a month, kissed me on the forehead, and dropped his briefcase on the kitchen table. "I'm going right to sleep," he said and headed toward the bedroom before I could say anything.

Now I see the outdoor light is still on, left burning for Kim's return, and the light in the hall too. Even so I stumble into things—a chair, a pair of wet boots. And the rain's still coming down hard, the same as when I went to bed. In the living room, I pick the receiver out of the dark.

"Kim?" he asks. "What took you so long? The whole house is probably up by now."

"No, it's Anna." I've never heard him like this before, almost angry. "Is that you Paul?"

"Yes." He hesitates, gathers breath. "Is Kim there?"

I stand by the phone shivering, trying to remember where my sister was going. She was wearing the heels she usually carries in a bag when she goes to work and a red dress she borrowed without asking just like she's always borrowed things. I buy clothes and she goes out in them before I even have a chance to wear them once. She left the closet open too, blouses slipping off the hangers. Maybe she didn't say where she was going. "I'm not sure," I say and cover the receiver, pretending to go look for her even though I feel silly. I don't know why I'm doing it. Her car keys jingled, swinging from her fingers as she went out the door into the rain. Then the screen door slapped shut, and I sat for two hours in the dark waiting for Barry to come home. Now I'm cold, tired, the whole house seems damp. I'm afraid the rain will wash it down the hillside. Or the bay will rise and swallow it—all this rain. Suddenly I'm mad at everybody.

"Anna, Anna," Paul is saying when I put my ear back to the phone. "Don't wake her. Please don't wake her," he says.

"I guess she's not in yet," I say.

"She's not? Isn't it sort of late?" He sounds upset. Who can blame him? "I just wanted to see how she was," he says. "Has she gotten my messages?"

In the light from the hall, I can see the last dark dozen roses he sent on the mantle, still in the plastic vase the florist brought them in. "She got all the flowers and letters," I say. I remember Kim and Barry were in the kitchen when the flowers came to the front door. As I bent to smell them, I could hear the two of them arguing over some small point, who should do the dishes or put the laundry in the dryer. The odor was heavy and sweet, palpable as a hand on my throat. I stopped, burying my face deeper and deeper in the flowers.

"I sent you something too," Paul says. "Did you get it? It's the last puppet in the set."

"Yes, we got him yesterday. He's wonderful. It's Rama, isn't it?" I've hung the shadow puppets flat against the living room wall, a frieze of brightly painted, cut-out figures, the perforated leather against the white like filigree. The prince, his wife Sita, and the other heroes, clowns, and giants from the Ramayana march in single file around the room.

19

"Yes, yes, it's Rama," Paul answers. "Kim always liked him the best. She thought he was really hot."

I hear him laughing a little, uncomfortably, trying to joke. In some far off distant past, I can remember Kim looking at some guy and saying, "You wouldn't think it, but what a stud!" Back when she used to talk to me about such things. I could tell Paul that Kim went out on a date but I don't really know for sure. And besides, it would only hurt him, not her. I think of all his sweetness, his letters and presents and phone calls. "I'm not sure when Kim'll be in," I say. "I think she might be at Mom's. Or maybe she said she was going out with Greta — her friend from high school? Should I tell her to call you?" I shift my weight from foot to foot.

"Well, I just wanted to see how she was — she's all right, isn't she?"

His voice sounds hollow, achy, and I worry about him again. "Of course. She's fine. She's been catching up with old friends, keeping herself busy."

"She's not too lonely?"

"I'm sure she misses you," I say. I don't think it's true, but it seems like the right thing to say. Light sweeps through the hall door, a bright triangle reaching almost to the sofa. The rest of the living room is black. I wind the phone cord around my fingers, tighter and tighter.

"I guess it's just as well she didn't come this time. She really wanted to come the first time, but she didn't end up liking it much," he says.

"Well, I had a great time," I say. Paul was researching the country's new immunization program for his public health degree, and Kim had gone with him. Her letters sounded cheerful, but once I was there I could see she was miserable no matter where we went, no matter what we did. In one village, we found a nurse giving shots to babies, and Paul and I went up to talk to her. The village was at the crown of a hill. All around, the rice fields dropped away in terraces, an unimaginable, saturated green that made the red earth at our feet sing in contrast. Each house had a carved lintel, fantastical signs and symbols I thought, protecting the inhabitants. While the children waited for their shots, Paul did tricks for them, pulling coins and birds and candy from behind their ears. The older kids came up to us, eager to talk and tell us jokes, and when I turned around, I was surprised to see Kim just pacing in the shade, slapping her thigh with her hat. Even there, where it was so beautiful, she seemed disgruntled. "I still don't understand why she was so unhappy," I say.

"You didn't have to live here with me," Paul laughs.

"I guess I didn't. But you didn't seem so bad to me." I remember that at one temple, the carvings seemed to be alive with monkeys hurling boulders into the sea, dancers tilting their heads and spreading their fingers, gods sporting the wings of eagles or the heads of elephants. In the middle of it all, Sita turned her voluptuous body to receive a messenger, bending her odd double-jointed elbows. Paul nuzzled Kim's neck and said, "She looks like you, just like you," but she pushed him away.

"Kim's not causing you any trouble, is she? She can be such a pain sometimes."

"Don't be silly, Paul."

"I'm just sorry I can't be there."

"Stop worrying. We go through this every time you call. You know everything'll be OK."

"OK," he says.

"This is costing you a fortune, Paul."

"I know, I know," he says, but he insists on staying on the phone. Is he waiting for Kim to walk through the door?

"I should go," I say, but I keep hearing him breathing and behind him, silence. He must be calling from some friend's fancy hotel room. I can see his forehead pressed against the air conditioned window, the dark hair, the shoulders bent. I can see him looking down on Jakarta, but I can't tell what he's thinking. I remember the kiss he gave me when I handed him his going away present—an umbrella decorated with frogs and lizards—and the way he backed toward the plane so he could keep us in sight as long as possible while Kim was already looking in her purse for the car keys. All these things I can infuse with meaning now, and life here rushes away from me at an incredible speed. Suddenly I need to keep talking to him. "It's raining cats and dogs here, but it's not cold any more," I blurt out. "We're all getting tired of being wet all the time. Except Barry—he just ignores it, he's so busy working. He settled that case he's been working on since September. No trial, so I think he was disappointed. He wouldn't say— he never does. But you know, he's always disappointed if he doesn't win the hard way."

21

"That's Barry," Paul says and laughs.

I laugh with him, but I get mad at Barry all over again. Just thinking about his calm, measured voice makes me mad. If I told Paul how I almost stole a little boy from a stroller in the supermarket, he'd laugh but he'd understand. If I told him the child looked like he came right from my gene pool, like he should be mine, Paul would know exactly what I meant; he wouldn't say, "Anna, you know that's illegal. If you want kids, just say so. You know I'm not against it," like Barry did when I came home that day. Then he rubbed my shoulders for a second, but his touch made me squirm. I hear the rain again outside, heavier now, hitting the carport roof with great force, and I think of Paul dashing in from the car. I think of him shaking the water from his hair, rain like silver beads in the porch light. After five years of drought, the rain just keeps coming. The hills up and down the Peninsula will be green through March and April, then by July everything will turn brown again if we don't all drown first. I could just leave, I think. I could just get on a plane and see Paul. "I miss you sweetie," I say very softly.

"What's that?"

"Nothing," I say and clear my throat. "We all wish you were home."

"Soon," he says. "I have to go now. Give Kim a big kiss for me."

When I hang up, the room seems very quiet, very dark. I'm shaking but it's not because I'm cold. I make it over to the couch and curl up in its corner, tuck my nightgown around my legs. I'm shaking because I'm thinking about my baby sister's husband, this sudden longing for him—or not so sudden longing. It didn't really catch me by surprise. Sometimes it's a question of when you acknowledge these things. Why do I keep that photo of Paul in my wallet anyway? In it, he's standing in front of a gray stone temple, step after step topped by bell-shaped stupas. His face has faded to an indistinct spot, but whenever I look at it, I remember how handsome he is. Next to him, Kim stands with her arms folded, her eyes, nose and mouth shaded by a wide-brimmed hat. I know she's scowling. That day at Borobudur was breathless with heat, silent, and the stones shimmered as I walked by them, fanning myself with a tourist brochure. On the walls, reliefs told the story of Buddha's life and insects hummed it too, in the fields and off in the distant trees. When I heard Paul and Kim arguing around the corner, I stopped, then stared and stared at the scene of Prince Siddharta's enlightenment, half afraid they'd hear my sandals on the terrace if I moved, half listening to their fight, my heart pounding. At the airport, waiting for my flight home, Kim told me she'd never been so lonely. "I just want to have a real conversation with someone in English," she said. "Someone other than Paul. He's never around and all he talks about is which villages have t.b. and which ones don't or which temple to go look at next. And I have these stupid fantasies about drinking water straight from the tap. I'm sick of all this exotic stuff."

I didn't know what to say because all I could think was how silly she was being, living some place where every day was as magical as this and wanting to leave. When she put her head on my shoulder, I hoped she was going to ask if she could use my plane ticket, if she could go back to the States, take care of the house and Barry and my job and leave me in Jakarta, but she only sighed. I looked over her bent head at Paul. He seemed oblivious, practicing card tricks, getting the whole deck to leap up into the air and vanish. Then he met my eyes, smiled, shrugged. I felt my face blaze, wondering if he could tell what I was thinking.

Now, outside, a car drives through the rain. Its headlights swing across the walls, then disappear. Back in Indonesia, I could go to another shadow play with Paul, sit in the dark and watch the shadows the puppets make—sharp and dark when the puppeteer sets the figures flush against the screen, diffuse when he moves them further away. The figures swoop and fight as the dalang chants the legend of Rama—how he was exiled to the forest for fourteen years before he could become king, how he was tricked by a demon in the shape of a golden deer and his beautiful wife Sita was stolen from him, how with the help of the white monkey Hanuman he was finally able to rescue Sita but couldn't believe she had remained faithful all those years. She threw herself on a pyre and emerged unscathed, a sign of her purity. The dalang lowers his voice and growls for the demons, lilts when Sita speaks. The shadows grow until they swirl around our knees, up around our chests. I feel Paul sitting very close to me, whispering translations in my ear. As he talks, he waves his

23

hands and I capture one and hold it very firmly between my knees until it stops struggling. I can feel his thumb on the inside of my knee, the weight of his arm. The closeness makes me dizzy. I shiver and remember I'm in my own living room, Paul miles and miles and miles away.

I hear Kim's car pull up, the silence when the engine dies, and the door being closed softly. I think how I should creep back to bed. I don't want her to find me here, waiting up for explanations the way our mother did, but I run into her in the hall.

"Anna," she says. "You're up."

"Paul called. I was just going back to bed."

"You weren't waiting up, were you?"

"He really misses you," I say and she looks exasperated. Then we both giggle when we hear Barry groan and smack the bed with his palm.

"Anna?" he says.

"Out here. I'm just talking to Kim." We hear him turn over, then she pulls me into the living room, turns on a light.

"I don't want you keeping track of me," she says. "This whole thing is my business."

"Don't you want to be there?" I say. "I mean, you're married to Paul, not to us."

"You don't know what you're talking about, Anna. You're blowing everything out of proportion. I'm here. He's there. That's all. We work it out when he gets back. OK? I went over there once with him and I hated it, remember?"

She starts taking off her coat, her shoes, and I remember how one day we went out stupidly at noon, and in the steaming Jakarta heat, Paul told story after story as we walked—how the government, deciding the streets were too crowded, had ordered half the city's rickshaws tossed into the harbor and never paid the owners. "That figures," Kim said grimly, but Paul and I laughed until we followed her gaze and saw a man bathing in the dirty water at the bottom of the sewage canal we were walking by. When we left for the countryside, escaping the petrochemical plants and diesel exhaust and dust, Kim seemed to breathe easier but only until the village kids swarmed up to her and all their small hands reached out to pinch her white arms. "Candy," they demanded. "Gula gula. Give me money." I only saw that they were laughing, teasing, and I found their demands weirdly amusing given the exotic beauty around them—the same way I responded to finding Madonna t-shirts for sale in all the stores—but Kim had a darker vision. "It's disgusting," she said, once her antagonism had scared all the children away. "It's so depressing it makes me cry," she said, but she couldn't explain what she meant.

She looks very tired now, and I realize how late it is, too late to be arguing. And it's true, when Paul comes back, she'll move out of our house, back in with him. They'll work it out or they won't. In any case, Paul won't throw her over because she stayed out late while he was away. "I guess you're right," I say.

"We're just different people, Anna," she says and hugs me before leaving the room.

The rain has softened to a delicate drumming, the whirr of wings in leaves. I sit and think how I'll go back to bed, keep my distance, lie there and listen to Barry breathing. I won't wake him up. I won't touch him, not tonight anyway. Years ago, Kim snuck up on us one afternoon as we napped in the backyard. She took a picture, a shot angled down on twisted clothes, a tangle of arms and legs, seamless, my head on Barry's chest and my hair spread out over the grass like a flag. Kim's giggling woke us or maybe it was the sudden cool of her shadow falling across our faces. On our first anniversary, she gave us the photo in an inlaid wooden frame she made herself. Sometimes I look at it and at the photo next to it, taken at Kim's wedding. In it, Paul looks lovingly down at my sister, and she seems to be smiling up at him. But, I wonder, maybe they were looking off at different, distant things even then.

In Indonesia they still tell stories from the Ramayana all the time: turn off the main street in Jogjakarta at night, Paul says, and you'll find a wayang, people seated on both sides of the screen from dusk to dawn watching the puppets, listening to the gongs of the gamelan, napping and waking again. People have been telling these same stories for a thousand years. That appeals to me—all that tradition to rely on—but I know that here you'd be crazy to think for an instant of throwing yourself on a pyre like Sita did. No magic could save you, it would prove nothing but your own foolishness, and there's nothing to prove here anyway except by living. I know that, here, things change slowly. No dramatic gestures.

25

Here, we talk and talk and end up believing that in a few days we'll see things differently; we'll be happy again. Or the argument continues until it peters out on its own, and we're left drained, standing on opposite sides of the room, and finally we look at each other, shrug, and agree everything's over, love a thing of the past.

I know all this, but still, when I turn out the light, I'm blinded by the filigreed silhouettes of the shadow puppets. Silver against black like photo negatives. They stretch their long, jointed arms and twist their heads on skinny necks, their hair like the airy curl of ferns. They dance and kick, swipe at each other, make love passionately, soar up the walls; I grasp at the fading image of their sharp noses, their shining eyes, and the parabolas of their smiles.

WANTING WHAT WE DON'T WANT

I HAVE A TWIN SISTER named Amelia. She wants to be alive and I want to be dead; otherwise we're identical. Born on the cusp of midnight, first me and then her—Wednesday's child is full of woe; Thursday's child has far to go. We shared the same tight space of the womb, we shared a placenta. In the middle of the night, she comes to me, black hair dripping around her pale face like a ghost, and she whispers, whispers, whispers as if she has no one else to talk to. As if I have no one else to listen to.

When we were five, she drowned and I didn't. We were both wearing white party dresses for a sunny Fourth of July—hers with a blue sash, mine with a red. At the same time, on a whim, we jumped from the pier into the cold water of the bay. I struggled up to the surface again, but a dark bottom monster grabbed onto her ankle in its white, lace-trimmed sock and wouldn't let go. Our mother says more likely her foot caught a piling and she couldn't rise or she gulped water like air and sank, but I know better: they never found her body because he'd eaten it, every last ribbon and bow. And for years I couldn't wear blue, the color of cold bay water, the color of death.

I kept asking: where is she? where is Amelia? when is she coming back? I kept imagining her regurgitated like Jonah from the whale. And when there were no answers I grew silent. I refused to wind the music box topped by a couple waltzing to "The Blue Danube." I ate only soft food. I wouldn't talk, so intent was I on being the first to hear her footsteps, to hear the cable car that brought her home. Our father took time from work; he held me, read to me, dragged me to the zoo where he steered me toward the dry land animals—

camels, zebras, lions—and away from the hippos wallowing in their muddy pool, away from the seals splashing from their blue-painted rocks into a phony sea. All the while he told stories to the air because I resisted listening; I was busy listening for something else. He talked and talked and the stories circulated above my head, but I remember only two of them—the one about the brave baby salmon who made it back up stream while a thousand of its compatriots died, and the one about baby sea turtles scrambling down toward the tide— how some of them were scooped up by hungry gulls but others reached the waves. On alternate days, our mother treated me to strawberry sundaes or bought me a whole new set of Legos which I'd only play with when the vacuum was running. Otherwise the plastic snap of the joining blocks made too much noise. The doctors told our parents that, being so young, I might express my grief in strange, unexpected ways. Because, they assured, I would grieve, I did understand that Amelia was gone for good. So the day I began to cry, the tears flooding me mysteriously as if some other little girl inside of me were crying, our mother smiled: one daughter was gone but the other had returned to the land of the living. Our father called his friends and business associates and told each of them how the tears had welled from my eyes and become a torrent. Five hours later, he was still talking and I was still crying. Finally our mother begged me to stop: "Oh my dear, don't cry so hard or you'll drown in your tears like Alice." The wrong thing to say: I imagined joining Amelia in a salty swim, a wet salty death.

The day I tore our room apart, she thought I was grieving too. I ripped bedding from the beds—top and bottom bunks. I spilled crayons and pastels, ground them into the carpet with the heels of my hands. Through a veil of mad tears, I saw the colors turn to mud. I tipped the doll house over, sending miniature bedroom sets and chandeliers crashing, breaking the tiny plates dolls eat off of. The day I slashed all Amelia's drawings from the walls and burned her baby blue angora sweater, our mother thought I was finally expressing my anger at my sister's desertion by destroying her things, and she cheered me on, joining in the mayhem even as she rushed for the fire extinguisher. But she didn't understand at all, not at all: I was freeing her, my sister, Amelia with wings.

Things we want: true love of course; Mama doing our hair up in braids and French twists; Daddy holding us in his lap, his hairy forearms crossed over our bellies; toe shoes and pink tulle skirts, tiaras and diamond rings; being able to shoot perfect free throws with our eyes closed; a daughter who does what she's told; Phi Beta Kappa keys to wear on gold chains around our necks and finger when we're nervous; a man who looks into our eyes and lets us do all the talking; a baby; a job where we file index cards all day—because we have enough to think about at home; a girlfriend who lends us her sweaters and we're exactly the same size; narrow hips; a man who tells charming stories all the time—until we realize they're all stories about himself; black leather jackets and packs of Marlboros to roll up in our t-shirt sleeves; Daddy incapacitated by old age until he can't talk anymore; a mother who doesn't hover; a flat chest and coat hanger shoulders so clothes fit us the way they fit fashion models; the clothes themselves— Armani, Missoni, Calvin Klein; a grandmother who teaches us to bake pie, then kicks off her shoes and complains about Grandpa's infidelities; multiple orgasms; an easy death, quiet in the night; a job where we get to make the decisions and people actually listen to us; sons instead of daughters because they'll love us better, because they'll take care of us in our old age; for the following adjectives to apply to us: voluptuous, luscious, lascivious, Rubenesque; the aloof look fashion models have even when they smile; bigger hips so when that baby comes, it can slide out easy; no children, no children at all; to be a U.S. Senator—gray-haired and distinguished; a mother who's not invisible; for our hair not to go gray until we're past our sexual prime—whatever that is; a daughter who's just like us but smarter, better, funnier, braver; a job where we can live in the same sweater and pair of jeans day in, day out; time before we die to say goodbye to everyone, even if it means struggling to breathe through hospital tubes; grandchildren to buy presents for; to be left alone, to be left completely alone; living longer than everyone we know now, so that only young people come to our funeral.

I get up and stand at the kitchen sink while he goes to answer the phone. A dark spring day, the room filled with harsh fluorescent light. He's hired me to redesign his house and I've fallen in love with him despite all my common sense,

29

despite the fact I know he'd be bad for me. Whenever I see him, I feel faint, I can't breathe. Whenever I think of him, I feel like a fool, a hopeful fool, waiting for the day he stops teasing me about dates I haven't had and asks me out on one himself or I get up the nerve to ask him out. I've fallen in love with him despite the fact he wants to take this beautiful, old, Victorian house and rip out the etched glass panels on either side of the front door, put in a sunken living room, track lighting and dimmer switches, wall-to-wall carpeting. He wants to rip up the parquet floor with its Greek-key pattern border, and turn the meandering upstairs rooms into two identical boxes. He lives on the dark side of a dark city and he wants to remove the bay windows, lessen the light even more. The house sits on a magnificent site, a bluff overlooking the river and the miles and miles of fields beyond it. You'd think the place would be filled with light, but the main rooms face north, and all fall and winter fog rises from the river until it blots out the sky. Those bay windows are his only chance to catch the sun, but he insists on a flat wall of glass, huge panes that will buck and shiver in the winter storms. It's clear he doesn't know the first thing about houses, and I've fallen in love with him anyway, even though my job is houses.

30

I welcomed him to our first meeting the way I welcome any client—a firm handshake, some conversational patter while he inspected the awards hung on my office walls and looked at models of my previous projects, before and after photos of earlier renovations, then a cup of coffee and down to the serious business of figuring out what he had in mind for his house.

"It's an old house," he said. "I like the location but not the house. Not all of the house anyway." He said that he liked the entryway that soared two stories and the long clean lines of the dining room, but there were far too many rooms for a single person and the place reminded him of visits to the grandmother from whom he'd inherited it.

"Ah," I said, "bad associations."

"It was like being sent to prison for the weekend," he said and regaled me with stories for an hour and a half. He described his grandmother, all 300 pounds of her, resting that heavy weight on the ornately carved banister as she shooed the grandchildren up to an early bed. He recalled the games he'd played with his older sisters while Grandma napped, snoring away in a red velvet parlor chair, the shades drawn down so tight their silk tassels touched the floor. In the dusty attic, he played the pupil while his sisters were the teachers, the patient while they were nurses, a tiger while they were ring mistress and animal tamer, whipping him into submission, telling him to sit on his own paws. "So that's it," he said. "I've inherited the damn place and I guess I can do what I want with it now that I have the money. Come and see it next week," he said. "You can take a look around, see if you think you can do something with it."

At the time, I thought nothing of it. At the time, I thought, "OK. He wants to modernize, add some windows, knock out a few walls, maybe put in a new bath and a restaurant quality range in the kitchen." At the time, I thought I could do the plans in a few days, write up the specs, call the contractors and get him a decent bid on the work, be out of there in no time. But now it's been months, and I'm being completely unprofessional. I'm working weekends, dragging things out. Other projects, more lucrative projects, are piling up on my desk because I've fallen in love with his easy, loping walk and the way he fingers the spot on his chin where he nicked himself shaving as if he's forgotten how it got there. Fallen in love with the color of his skin, bluish as skim milk, and with his blond hair in tight cherubic curls. Fallen in love with the definiteness with which he states, "Take that wall down, and that one, and that one," until I wonder how the house will continue to stand.

All winter we've met every other week over plans and coffee at his kitchen table. He's hired me but he won't listen to a thing I say, so I make suggestions gently. After all, he's a beginner at this, I tell myself, just a guy who's gotten rich unexpectedly, who's good at something else but not at designing houses. If I'm too tough on him, I'm afraid he'll never love me back; I'm afraid the hand that holds a pencil and drives black marks across my plans, the fingers with their nails bitten bloody (I tell myself their vulnerability exposes the lie of all his arrogance) will never touch my cheek.

At the end of the day, I go home to Maxi stretching her wrinkled green iguana neck for another grape. She'd prefer a sunnier clime, one without all this fog and dark, but at least I leave the gro-light on for her all day. There are two messages on the machine—one long distance from my mother and the

31

other a bad dirty limerick from the last guy I dated. The last guy before I fell in love with the house wrecker and went into hiding, carrying his image around with me everywhere like a golden amulet in my heart. Before going to bed, I fold underwear—pink, green, and black panties, bras I've dyed to match. I can't wear pink under black jeans, black under a red sweater; it's impossible, I itch all day. I imagine him undressing me, peeling off a gray sweater to find a pewter camisole underneath. In the middle of the night, I wake up in a sweat, aware how foolish I'm being. I get up and walk around the apartment, slapping my hand down on furniture and windowsills, thinking that this isn't what I struggled through physics and calculus for, this isn't why I did four years of grad school and three years of apprenticeship, suffered through seven licensing exams. I'll tell him his plans to redesign his house make me sick; I'll tell him they'll ruin this house, and besides they're trendy ideas from 20 years ago (really, a sunken living room!); I'll tell him that if he wants a sleek modern house he should buy one or build one—I'll even design it myself—but that he should not, under any circumstances, alter this Victorian with its coffered ceilings and separate water closet and wrap-around porch. I open the blinds and stare out at the dark city, shrouded in midnight, mid-winter fog but I <u>see</u> his house—red with blue trim, its gables and turrets poised over the river. Before I fall asleep again, I imagine that when I say all this, he will open his arms, pull me toward him in joy.

32

Today when I see him, though, I keep my mouth shut. I lay the plans out on his kitchen table and know, as I've known all along, that I shouldn't have taken this job. As soon as I saw what he wanted, I should have bowed out—but that was the same moment I fell in love. I stand over him, looking down at the way the hair curls along the nape of his neck. He's glancing at the newest set of plans and I manage to mumble, "You know, you could change this house without completely destroying its character." When he says, "No. I don't think so," I've been given yet another chance to walk away, but I don't. I sit down. I become practical and efficient, and I josh around with him while we plan where all the new bathrooms will go. I tell myself that what he thinks about houses isn't really important compared to everything else— it's his house after all—and my heart aches but just a little because I remind myself that building a house for someone, a house in which they feel at home, can be an act of love. And because he smiles every time he looks at me.

We're sitting at his kitchen table and he's just told me he wants to retile the counters a magnificent cobalt blue, he wants to put a skylight over the table. "Yes," I say, "Oh, yes." I'm happy, I can feel myself glowing—he's finally agreed to a suggestion I made weeks ago. "He likes it," I think. "He likes it. He likes it." Then when the phone rings, he gets up to answer it, and I get up too and stand at the sink and look out the window into his backyard and breathe and breathe. There's a high fence and most of the yard is paved concrete, but along the back wall all sorts of trees and bushes grow in a strip of earth. The plum trees have just started blooming. I look at the plum blossoms and I'm happy because I think how he's made a good choice; the kitchen will be beautiful. I imagine eating meals at the table, sunlight falling on our heads. I look at an old man pruning one of the rose bushes and I look at a huge vine in the corner that might be bougainvillea and I'm just waiting for him to come back.

So he gets up and excuses himself and answers the phone in the next room with the same jocular tone he's been using with me. "Yo," he says, "Bobby here." Then his voice drops the way men's voices always do when they talk to their girlfriends on the phone, and I hear him say, "Aw Baby, don't tell me that." It's the last thing I hear, the very last thing. I feel the floor slip away and a chasm opens up in front of me, black and very deep. It spreads and swells so that I need to clutch the edge of the sink with both hands to keep from falling in. Out the window, all the colors swim together, green mostly; then the fog turns everything gray, drizzle or rain or tears, but I know I'm not crying, not over this idiot. It's just that my stomach turns and the room twists and spins until everything is black, a black so deep it's squeezed all sound and color and light out of the world. I'm blind but I keep hearing his voice drop off into some other woman's ear, the way an echo falls down a cliff into total silence, and suddenly all I can think of is Barbara Bel Geddes in *Vertigo*, shoving her fingers through her hair and saying, "Stupid. You're so stupid," to herself over and over while Jimmy Stewart walks out the door to find the glamorous and sorrowful and mysterious woman he's really in love with. I know I'm feeling sorry for myself, but I keep

33

tipping and sliding and saying, "Stupid. You're so stupid. Of
course he's seeing someone," over and over again like a mantra
to keep from falling into the abyss—to keep from being
swallowed up by the darkness and the smell of damp plaster
like someone a long time ago pissed on an old wall. I can't see
anything. It can't be bougainvillea, I think. Bougainvillea
doesn't grow here. Where I grew up, fog tumbles over the
hills and out across the bay every afternoon at four and pulls
back the next morning at eleven, just exactly as if someone
were pulling at a sheet with a giant hand. Behind it, the sky is
the solid dense blue of a frescoed wall, and then the
bougainvillea flowers, like paper lanterns, start to glow. Here
fog rises from the river and the damp fields, the dark milky
color of water an India Ink brush has been rinsed in. It rises at
night while I'm sitting down to dinner or hunching over work
that must be completed for a meeting the next day. Maybe for
the last hour before sunset, say from four to five, it thins a
little and if I look straight up, I can see some watery sky, but
the chill never leaves. There's not enough light for
bougainvillea to grow here; that vine must be something else.

   34   The back door slams, and the gardener comes in, leaving
his muddy shoes on the step outside. He's an old Japanese
man, wearing a straw hat even in the rain. His socks shuffle
on the linoleum. I'm still sniffling, tasting salt on my lips.
Then he turns, comes up to me, looks in my face. "You look
like you seen ghost," he says. "You OK?"

   "Yes, I'm fine," I say, surprised I don't start crying again.
Then he shuffles into the living room with his hat on. I'm still
listening for the man's voice, waiting for it to soar, holding
my breath, and suddenly I feel all the blood rush into my face.
I say, "Fuck this! Just fuck this!" I say it out loud. I don't care
if anyone hears me. I unclench my hands—they're stiff from
holding onto the edge of the sink—and look out the window
again. The old man only has a strip of garden to tend but he's
balanced the two plum trees beautifully against the gray fence;
its silvery color offsets the show of their pale pink blossoms.
Later in the year, roses will bloom, huge and fragrant, and the
bougainvillea—or whatever it is he's chosen to plant--will
cascade down the wall in the corner, a magenta waterfall. I've
been given a whole house to work with—what will I do with
it? That's what's important.

In real life, there are a dozen endings possible, variations of mood, event, emotion. But as a story, it has to end here, right when she recognizes the old man's dignity and her own lack of dignity, right when she accepts the fact that she's not willing to sell out anymore—before the man she's in love with comes back into the room and ruins everything. In real life, when the man I'm in love with comes back into the room, he's just as handsome as ever, just as charming. He still smiles at me and touches my shoulder, and even though I know this flirtation is meaningless, probably the way he looks at every woman, I'm still in love with him. I'm mad at myself and embarrassed, but I still want his voice to be filled with longing when he talks to me on the phone as if he's trying to touch something through the wires—not when he talks to that other woman. In real life, I won't know until the words come out of my mouth whether I'll tell him to take his business elsewhere, to take his sly smiles and lanky walk, to take his childhood stories and the sweet smell of his clean clothes, and find another architect, because I'm not going to do it, I can't do it, I can't smash those bay windows flat against the walls the way you stomp on eggshells with a heavy boot. I can't ruin this house, not even for love. In real life, I don't know whether I'll do this or whether we'll argue for hours about fenestration, ornamentation, and ceiling fixtures and end up friends, or whether I'll just sit down next to him and tell him the blue tiles and skylight and glass doors on the cabinets are great ideas—because they are, after all—whether I'll praise him for an idea that was originally mine, because it doesn't matter whose idea it was if the house ends up beautiful, if he ends up loving me. In real life, I may very well go home, take all the dusty wineglasses from the cupboard and hurl them down at the kitchen floor, imagining that I'm throwing them at his head, then appear at work the next morning dressed in a suit fresh from the dry cleaners. I don't know whether to stand over him and explode in a glorious burst of righteousness or whether to sit down and dare to move closer.

35

Our mother knows what to do; Amelia is certain. Our mother whispers, "He's not good enough for you," but Amelia says, "Yes. Scream. Throw things. Cry your eyes out. Send him packing. Yes, yes, oh yes. Move closer." She's got a file full of stratagems she's picked up from *Cosmo* and *Mademoiselle*.

"Make sure he sees you looking at him, then look away for thirty seconds before looking back," she says. "It's a sure way of letting a man know you're interested." First one, then another, then none of these seem like the answer to my question so I sit and twist the words this way and that until they spin in my head like a carousel — all that jangling music — and I can't figure out how they'll sound when they come out, if any of them will make me happy.

The first time I wrote this, the man was trying to write his autobiography and the narrator had been hired to help him — a ghost writer. The first time I wrote this, she didn't love him at all; he made her scream with anger and frustration; she murdered him. The first time I wrote this, it was about my own twin sister who was still-born. The first time I wrote this, it was about my twin daughters, one of whom was still-born. It was about my twin daughters who are five now, alive and healthy, a real handful. Stars spin over the trees at night, constellation following constellation. Petals unfold — dogwood and poinsettia, the real blossom inside a set of showy bracts which we persist in thinking of as the flower. Chinese boxes. Russian dolls. How many things here are lies? How are they true?

Where Amelia lives, they do the shopping on Monday, the baking on Tuesday. On Wednesday they dust, garden on Thursday, wash clothes on Friday, and iron on Saturday. They follow the same careful arrangement of chores every week. Where Amelia lives, they woke up at dawn last Friday, peered out the pantry window on the way to putting a load of whites in the washer, and found their cars coated with a fine sticky dust, almost as if mud had fallen from the sky and dried. But this substance was a light beige, a color like no earth anyone had ever seen anywhere, in any of their previous lives. It had a slightly pink tinge, and then when it got wet, turned a pale mauvish brown. Mysteriously, it had fallen only on cars, not on lawns or sidewalks. The rhododendron leaves were still the same shiny green as always. In all the window boxes, the geraniums still flamed a brilliant red. By mid-morning, the authorities hadn't finished their testing, and everyone was starting to taste something in the backs of their throats, like ash from a distant fire where bodies are being burned. Amelia

36

came to me Friday night and that's what she said. She said they'd been told to breathe softly and there was no telling how long it would last. Where Amelia lives, this may be the only thing to bother them for ages on end—an odd taste in the backs of their throats. They wait patiently for it to go away. They don't cry there, you know, even when their lovers walk out the door without a backward glance, even though they suspect they're breathing the desiccated remains of the ones they loved a long time ago. In her cocoon of long dark hair, Amelia tries to cry but she can't. She chops onions but the result is unsatisfactory, a purely physical reaction, not what she wanted at all. She tries to think of sad things: babies lost in shipwrecks, the carnage of a plane crash, wars, floods, famine. She thinks of things closer to home: our father's death at the age of forty-four, the sudden heart attack he had while hiking and the way his eyes glazed over, staring up at the blue sky over Yosemite's Half-Dome; our mother racing down the pier when she heard our splash and then standing there stunned and shivering in her party clothes, the silver fish scale pants and the silver halter top. Amelia even tries to feel sorry for herself, imagining the life she could have had. But all the emotions are fleeting, not steady enough to bring on a single tear, and she tells me she goes back to her sheets, slung across the ironing board with the dense wet weight of dead birds.

When I wake up the next morning, it's still dark. When I wake up I'm crying, but the tears taste sweet as well as salt. Chocolate-covered pretzels were Amelia's favorite food, a combination you can't imagine will taste good but it does.

First Trimester

I'm lying here tied to this bed, not really tied, not by irons or chains or ropes or shackles. So not really tied and it's not a bed but a couch, not a bed of straw in a dungeon even if it feels that way sometimes. It's a couch in a nice living room with a fireplace and cool blue walls we painted together right after we moved in and a giant screen TV Marco just bought for me—an extra special Christmas present just for this occasion. Because I'm tied to this bed by our baby. I'm fertilized, impregnated, I'm in a delicate condition. I want to have this baby. Yes, I do. No, I don't. I don't want to have this baby. I don't. I want to.

I'm tied to this bed by pain, pain from this baby. It's pinching nerves, pressing on them, sitting on them so I can't move. No, I know it can't really sit yet, not at this stage. It just swims like a tadpole in a pond. Sciatica—nerve like a line of fire from the hip into the thigh, a string pulled tight, a needle, six hundred pins. From the French *sciatique*, I looked it up. From Old French and back and back, from Medieval Latin *sciaticus*, alteration of Latin *ischiadicus*, from Greek *iskhiadikos, iskhias, iskhiad-,* sciatica, from *iskhion*, the hip. I can't have an operation cause it's too risky. I can't go to a chiropractor cause God knows what he'd turn around. I could find an acupuncturist but the insurance won't pay. And I can't take drugs cause they'll hurt the baby—not aspirin or Advil or Tylenol even. "Well," the doctor said, "a Tylenol once in a while won't hurt." He smiled and patted my shoulder. I'd have laughed at him but I was in too much pain. The insurance will pay for drugs all right—Codeine, Demerol, Morphine—but I can't take those, my doctor says I can't take those cause they'll hurt the baby, they will if I take them long term. I'll have a baby with two heads or no arms or a hole so we can see into the stomach like that cow they keep around here for the Ag students to study and the school kids to visit, and then what'll I do? Damaged goods, damaged property. And that's one thing no one wants—a damaged baby. They won't even buy one cheap.

"Baby, baby, baby," my husband says when he comes home from work and it's time for the backrub, the footrub, and the kisses. "Baby, baby, baby," Marco croons, feeding me whole grain muffins and bright green spinach and broiled chicken and anything else I can stand to swallow. When I beg for ice cream he pets my hair. "Now, you know that's bad for you," he says. "How about some nice strawberries all whipped up with yogurt. I got them special; they're not in season you know." But that frothy pink color makes me sick, that feeling I fight all day, like my stomach will bubble right out of my mouth, even if I nibble those crackers we leave on little plates by every chair and by the bed for when I wake up in the middle of the night. "Give me those berries and I'll puke," I say. But then I eat my bread and vegetables and chicken like a good girl. He cooks for me at the end of his own long day and how much more can I ask for? I smile and I mean it even though I dream ice cream, ice cream, ice cream. I hallucinate it: chocolate with a cherry, whipped cream too. But I can't have it cause gaining too much weight's bad for the baby—and me sitting here, lying here, tied to this bed, I'm not exactly getting any exercise. I can't feel it yet but I picture it rolling around in there, little salamander, getting enough exercise for both of us. I say to it, "I'm eating for two, you exercise for two, and we'll get a treat." We'll have that half glass of champagne on New Year's Eve the doctor promised us; it's just three days away. Come on, Baby, we'll listen to Christmas carols together—peace on earth, good will toward men—all that crap.

I'm so organized we were prepared for everything in the lab, every damn thing except this one. We had a foot stool so I wouldn't strain my back. We had a chair on wheels so I could roll around with ease. We had a grounded filter on the computer screen to block out radiation. We'd isolated everything possibly dangerous. And of course there were dangerous things—those birds had been washing up on the shores of the Salton Sea for almost two years. And even the

39

dead ones—who knew what might still be living in them, what had killed them? Mostly, I'd be working in my office anyway, supervising, writing, overseeing the work through that glass window reinforced with chicken wire. And for two months it was fine. Now I try to work at home. Carol drops reports off for me to review but the numbers swim on the page like little minnows. She calls with questions only I can answer, but I just say, "Yes, sure, go ahead with that. Sounds good," and I know she has to go ask someone else. I can't work. I can't follow the line of an argument. I can't spot the flaw that's upsetting the test. Oh baby, you little worm, you pest, you damn barnacle, get me through this somehow.

I know babies really can't do anything for you; they're too little to do anything except scream and cry and shit and eat and that's why we're supposed to love them—because there they are, helpless, and we can help them grow up into something great or at least into "whoever they want to be"; we can give them love, we can give them freedom. Until one of them gets pregnant and the baby starts sitting on the nerve that runs down into her leg and the nerve turns into a prison— just like bars of fire, just like an electrical wire. If I lie just right, with a pillow under my knee, it doesn't hurt so much but then the calf cramps and the muscle there turns into a stick of dynamite. I have to sit up and squirm and scream and massage it and that sets the nerve on fire again. But I can't take drugs cause that might hurt the baby. And I wouldn't want to be responsible for that.

But I do want this baby. I do I do I do, I say when the nerve knits up again. I say it in time to the throbbing. I've waited a long time for this, watching those other mothers with their sweet-faced infants in the grocery store, watching the relatives coo over every tiny cousin. I've waited a long time to have a little girl and dress her in Baby Dior rompers, and later velvet dresses and matching ribbons for her hair. A little girl to buy Barbie dolls for and those baby dolls that drink from a bottle and piss so you have to change the diapers. A little girl to take to ballet lessons so she can wear a tutu that shows off her chubby thighs and take to flute lessons and later she can go to cooking class. No—a little girl to take to the library and stack up piles and piles of books for her to read: Nancy Drew, *The Railway Children*, *Alice in Wonderland*. A little girl to play chess with, to collect moths by their silky wings and tadpoles in a jar. I think about all these plans when the pain gets really bad—like razor blades and bowie knives, carving knives, machetes, switchblades and bayonets cutting me til the blood comes. That's what it feels like, hot blood running up and down my leg. I think how this little parasite embedded in me will finally disengage.

On the ultrasound, it just looks like shadows. Feeding on me. "I positively think that ladies who are always enceinte quite disgusting; it is more like a rabbit or guinea-pig than anything else and really it is not very nice," Queen Victoria said, despite her nine children. I could stop eating I guess; I could eat more, I guess, make it grow faster, get this over with. Ovum and sperm, zygote, blastula and embryo, fetus shaped like a chicken. That's where we are now. Some sort of Frankenstein monster, some sort of Caligula, some sort of Godzilla, some Thing I can't even imagine—the Creature from the Black Lagoon, Rosemary's baby. Look at a monkey, you'll have a monkey. Slap your stomach and your baby will have a birthmark shaped just like a hand. I keep dreaming about being trapped in a tunnel, sunk in a lake of slush with a baby the size of Mount Olympus. I keep telling myself ribosome, nucleus, cytoplasm, chromosome; little fetus, that's all you are.

I keep waiting to get misty-eyed like my friends. If you don't do it, you'll miss it. If you don't do it, you'll be sorry. It'll hold your marriage together; it'll split your marriage apart. Ah, Marco. "Where's my baby? When's my Baby going to give me a baby?" he said. He said, "If you don't do it, you'll miss out on the mystery of life." Women, we're supposed to be closer to it, to that mystery of life. We're in tune with the moon and the tides, cycles, out of historical time, magical and mysterious and paradoxical, closer to nature. Lying here, I've never been further from it. I can look out the window all right, stare at the dirty melting snow. I can listen to the rain ding on the metal awnings. I can count and count and count the Christmas lights on the house across the street. I can watch the fog clear in the morning so I can see the clouds build up, put my hand against the glass and feel the cold. At the lake, great inland sea, it's never cold; it's hot and dry around that slick sheet of salty water, brush growing up its sides, and the sky is blue. You take the train down from Indio, down down below sea level and off in the distance you can see the

41

Chocolate Mountains, the Superstition Mountains, Rabbit Peak. Even with a hundred and fifty thousand dead birds washed up on the shores, it was beautiful. I open my eyes and it's raining here again, one damn drop after another. They'd kill for this water down there, those fools. Maybe it's just that I'm in pain, maybe it's just that I'm in pain.

SECOND TRIMESTER

Nobody wants a damaged baby, except for those Mother Theresa types you see on TV—and I see a lot of TV—who adopt fifty AIDS babies and nurse them until they die. I know we're all supposed to be like that—give up for our babies because they "give us so much, so much love." But this baby isn't doing anything for me except giving me the time to watch a lot of TV, except giving me the excuse to build another room onto the house, except giving my mother an excuse to come out and visit me, except—because of the pain—giving me an excuse to scream a lot and moan a lot and cry whenever I want to and have her or Marco come and put cold rags on my forehead. All those things you can't do out in the street or the office. Try moaning out loud on the bus and see what happens.

My mother gave up everything for me. She wore my old underwear with the elastic stretched out so I could get silk ones. She wore my old socks, the ones with holes in the heels, so I could buy stockings. She cooked nineteen thousand meals for me before I left home for college and insisted I eat everything she put on my plate. She vacuumed my room nine hundred and thirty-six times, took me in for ten sets of shots, wiped innumerable bloody knees, shrieked countless times when she found my failed science experiments—bananas left under the bed to rot, field mice deprived of food to see how long they'd last, every household cleanser mixed together to force some sort of explosion. And now she's here taking care of me since I can't sit or stand for more than an hour. "So, you finally got knocked up," my father said, chuckling, when I told him he was going to be a grandfather. "Well, we waited long enough. You've been married ten years. I was beginning to wonder, but hey, listen, take care of yourself you hear, and now here's your mother. I know she'll want to talk to you." "I'm pregnant," I said to her when she got on the phone. "The bloody thing keeps tweaking my sciatic nerve. It's killing me."

42

She's been here two months now, from the end of January, when it became clear Marco and I couldn't do this alone. When she came, she brought books for me. She brought *Helpful Hints for Your Pregnancy* and *The Well Baby Book, A Child Is Born, What to Expect When You're Expecting*. She brought *Be Pregnant, Be Beautiful*. We've read them all but none of them give more than a sentence to sciatica. They pass it off as a possible inconvenience, the way the doctor says, "Now this may pinch a little," right before he drives a needle into your arm. And we've spent days coming up with lists and lists of unlikely baby names. It's taken weeks to get from the ordinary — Jennifer, Patrick — to the odd — Cimmarron, Eugenides. She came with me and Marco to the ultrasound and the amnio, got teary-eyed as we all watched the blood pumping through those tiny veins. Weeks and weeks she's been here, and now she's seen all the damn trees blossom, the crocuses and daffodils come up, and the tulips start to lose their petals. Next she'll see the rhodies bloom in front of every house, identical rhodies and azaleas in front of identical three bedroom split-level ranch styles, the same pinks and reds and oranges everywhere because the deer won't eat them. Every afternoon, she takes her umbrella and goes for a brisk walk up to campus. She walks around my lab building and reports back to me. When she's feeling particularly peppy, she insists I hobble out to the carport and smell the air, even though the rain drips off the overhang right onto my head. "Breathe, breathe, breathe," she says, and she stands up straight and takes the air in deep like she's setting an example for a two year old. Like I'm only bent over with pain cause I want it that way. "Smell that springtime smell," she says. Then she starts humming. I know she doesn't mean it. I know she's being really nice to me but I don't want to be nice to her. I don't want to be nice to anyone. She even lets me scream when the pain gets really bad. Or I tell her that's why I'm screaming but really it could be anything — maybe it's the fact that my friend can call up and talk about *The Brady Bunch* for hours and I can talk about them with her — they're back in, they're back on Nickelodeon, they're back in a movie. Maybe it's the fact that my mother and I watch Donna Reed's perfectly run household on TV every day and then we watch 99 in *Get Smart* with her little suits and matching hats even when she's pregnant, neat little outfits in a hounds-tooth check. I have to watch her when I use up my hour showering and getting into a clean pair of sweatpants in the morning. Then it's flat on my back until the pain goes away. Maybe it's the fact that it's been raining for months straight. I watch it out the window: gray milk, gray sludge, gray mud, gray ash, gray slush, gray slime. I start saying gray, gray, gray, gray, gray. It takes my mind off the pain. "That pain should be gone by now," the doctor said, "but I guess you're carrying low. Perfectly natural though. Don't you worry about a thing. That baby's perfect, by the way. The tests came back and there's nothing wrong with Baby."

When we get home, my mother says, "Let's watch that TV show set in Hawaii and we can imagine it's sunny here too. I'll move all the plants in here, that nice palm you have in the bedroom. We'll close the curtains and turn up the sound extra loud so we can pretend we're in Hawaii too. You'll like that, won't you?" So we turn it on and watch Jacques Lord, El Mas Macho, and Book-em-Danno run around being tough and then they bust some poor shmuck who's running drugs in order to support some leftist political cause. I keep trying to see around the people, just look at the scenery—looking for beaches and oceans with big waves, mountains covered with rain forest, waterfalls, and maybe a volcano about to blow—but even when I can see around the people, all I see are high rises and cars from the 70's (big Impalas, and Cadillacs), maybe a city bus. Local color means girls in hula skirts and flower bras who you look at but never talk to and they're always smiling. What drugs are they on? I think. When it's over, my mother says, "Now isn't that better?" "Sure," I say. Yeah sure, I think. Let's watch it again tomorrow. It's on every afternoon at two, a TV trip to a tropical paradise where the hero wears a suit that looks too small. He has an unbending set of wrinkles and hair slicked in place with nitroglycerin and contraceptive jelly. "Hey, we can watch *Gilligan's Island*," I say. "That's set on a tropical island too," but my mother says, "No, I can't. Those people are too stupid even for me to watch," and we both laugh. She's OK sometimes, I think. I think I shouldn't be so hard on my mother anymore. I should have gotten over this. I should have gotten over how she wore the same winter coat for fifteen years while I was growing up so I could keep getting new ones.

She's flipping through the channels and she finds *Star Trek: The Next Generation* where there are women starship captains but they're always the captain of some other ship. "Now that

Counselor Troy," my mother says, "she's got real woman's intuition. See, in the future they'll recognize how important that is." She reaches over and pats my hand and I think, Jesus Christ, I used to be a biologist but I can't remember anything, anything at all. I used to be able to think! What's happening to me? In the middle of the night, I wake up and I can't remember if we tested for avian cholera yet or avian botulism, how much selenium we found in their livers, how much mercury, how much chromium, how many birds have died. Jesus, I can barely remember that DNA is a double helix. All I can remember is: this is when the baby develops fingerprints, this is when the baby's eyes open; this is how much vitamin A to take, how much niacin, how much folic acid; this is how Samantha does her tricks—she wiggles her nose—and this is how Jeannie does hers—she crosses her arms and blinks her eyes. I keep dreaming about those damn birds, floating in some liquid suspiciously like amniotic fluid, and I break into a sweat. When I wake up I remember they're in the Salton Sea; it _is_ like amniotic fluid. I call Carol and she says, "Don't worry. Just relax. We're doing fine here. And your name's still going on that article as lead author. Just stop worrying. It'll all be waiting for you when you come back. Those dead birds aren't going anywhere." I think of a hundred and fifty thousand grebes belly up in the Salton Sea, with their pointy bills and ruby eyes and vestigial tails and the fleshy membranes along their toes. Those clumsy bastards, they can't make it on land. They say a little confusion is normal—leaving the house without keys, misplacing your purse. They say to slow down, make lists, check the items off—pick up dry cleaning, get dog groomed. They say to post notes on the inside of the front door—is the stove off? Is the answering machine on? But what if you can't leave the house? What if you're tied to the house? What if the baby sits on your sciatic nerve and just won't move?

45

I put the phone down and my mother says, "What's the problem, honey?" I say, "We were talking about Connie Chung announcing to the world that she's taking time off from work so she can get pregnant. Isn't that ridiculous?" I ask. "What's it like, giving birth?" I ask.

"Oh wonderful dear," my mother says, "I got you in the end, the best thing I ever did." I think how my friend Marcia said, "Yup, great, just like getting run over by a Mack truck," but then a month later she said, "Oh, I never said anything like that, I'd never. You're making it up. It's not that bad."

"You're shitting me," I say to my mother. I turn on my side even though that makes it hurt more, even though that sends a spasm rocketing through my leg, ricocheting from hip to knee to toe. There's a coil wound tight and pulling tighter, and I feel the baby move. I've been feeling it for a while now, "quickening" they say, the fluttering and hopping and kicking. I try to decipher what it's saying, like Morse Code. Maybe it's telling me a secret; maybe it's teaching me a language only the two of us can understand; maybe it's telling me to get my act together. Then it kicks me in the ribs, sticks an elbow God knows where, wherever that damn nerve starts its flaming journey, and I'm off for an afternoon of bitching and groaning.

"I just don't know what to do with you when you get like this," she says, and when Marco comes home she meets him at the front door and tells him I had a pretty good day until "That woman Carol Something called from her work, got her all upset. She should be happy and look at her—she's like this instead." I can just see her throwing her hands up in exasperation.

When Marco comes over, I say, "Go away, you fucker. You got me into this mess in the first place." I can hear my mother clucking in the background but Marco just says, "OK baby, OK baby. It's good practice for what I'll hear during labor. Might as well get used to it." He chuckles, but he won't take his fucking hand away from my hip even though I can swear the heat from his fingers is making the pain worse, razor sharp darts when he pats pats pats.

The other day I almost fainted, stood up to go to the bathroom and felt so dizzy I had to sit right back down. "Head between the legs," my mother shouted and pushed my head down with her hand. I called the doctor because I was scared. "A little dizziness is normal at about this time," he said. "Don't you worry about it. It just means there's a little less blood going to your brain, but the baby will be fine." When he hung up, I really did put my head between my knees. When I was twenty-two I went to my mother's gynecologist with a vague pain somewhere near my left hipbone, cramping periods, sharp stabs when someone screwed me from behind (but I didn't tell him that last one). He stuck his gloved hand up inside me and felt around like he was testing tomatoes at the market, looking for perfectly ripe ones. The whole time I stared at the ceiling where they'd plastered a poster of two adorable kittens. The whole time the nurse made sure the modesty sheet covered my knees. Later, when I was dressed, the doctor looked at me like he didn't recognize me. Then he looked at some notes he'd made. He said, "Cysts on the ovaries. We'll have to do some tests, possibly operate." I swallowed hard and my hands began to shake. "But I'm going to Hudson Bay," I said. "We're leaving next week." I'd finished the first year of grad school and my professor was taking me to Canada for the summer to help her study geese. "You'll have to put it off. If we operate it could be a long recovery," he said. "I know you're upset because your plans have been disrupted, but what could be more important than your reproductive health?" His hands were folded in that fatherly way on the table. His white coat was immaculate, fat as a gander's belly. He leaned forward and said conspiratorially, "Nothing's more important than that, is it now?" How could I say it wasn't the most important thing to me? Later, I realized I could have died. It could have been ovarian cancer and not benign cysts. But he didn't say that. He didn't say, "Listen, young lady, this is serious, really serious. You could die here." He didn't say, "There's nothing more important than your health."

I can't be making this up, can I? It really was Demi Moore naked on the cover of *Vanity Fair* looking like a goddamn Madonna with one hand over her breasts and the other holding up her huge belly, and everybody arguing: she shouldn't have done it; yes, she should have done cause it's beautiful. Then with the next baby, just as big, they did her up in black lingerie and high heels, but nobody argued about that because she wasn't naked, you see. And then Courtney Love—denizen of Hole, guitar smashing punk band—couldn't be outdone. She got herself into *Vanity Fair* too, a picture of her pregnant belly, her swollen breasts—said she's gonna stop doing heroin cause it's bad for the baby, said pregnancy's been so good for her acne she didn't even have to have her pictures air-brushed. And she's right, you know, despite everything, this pregnancy's been wonderful for my skin; I'm fucking glowing. Sophie Tolstoy wrote in her diary, "I am nothing but a miserable, crushed worm, whom no one wants, whom no one loves, a useless creature with morning sickness, and a big

47

belly, two rotten teeth, and a bad temper, a battered sense of dignity, and a love which nobody wants and which nearly drives me insane," and she didn't even have to think about underwear with an elastic panel or an entire industry based on pre-natal vitamins. The linea nigra and red palms and the mask of pregnancy. We're talking indigestion and anemia, bleeding gums and varicose veins, leg cramps and hemorrhoids and edema. I'm retaining water, the doctor says, my feet plump as pigeons, fingers fat as Ballpark franks, Texas hots, pigs in blankets. 90% water—is that all we are? Water and a fetus with thin shiny skin? Oh baby, rosy piglet, little thing.

THIRD TRIMESTER

Oh, am I heavy, big with a bun in the oven, sick of my confinement—that's what it's called, you know. The pain's gone now but every day that belly gets bigger, and just when I thought all that simmering and sizzling and lying around was over, I'd be able to get in a couple of good months work before the baby came and my mother could go home, my cervix shortened and I felt two brief pangs that could have signaled premature labor. "Back to bed with you, young lady," the doctor said. I lie here and say, "Baby, you can come out now. It's OK. You can breathe out here now. Come on already, let's get this over with. I've had enough," I say. "It hasn't exactly been a picnic for me either, you know," my mother says every time I gripe. "You haven't been the nicest person to get along with these past five months." "Maybe I have something to bitch about," I call after her as she retreats to the kitchen.

Outside, I hear some college boys saying, "Don't diss me, babe," when a woman doesn't answer their catcalls. The rain's finally stopped—just like it does here every first of July—and the sun's come out hot and steamy. She's wearing shorts and sandals and a tank top. When she crosses the street, they hoot after her as if she's put on those clothes just for them. On TV I saw how some man in Boston killed his pregnant wife and blamed it on two black kids, and the world believed him for a long long time. On TV now, everyone in this little town is learning French by watching TV. They're all saying, "Le mouton est blanc," and outside there are real sheep looking in the barbershop windows but the people don't even see them.

I think how if this baby's a boy and we get into a war somewhere—some war in our national interest—he could get drafted and then get killed. Along the way, he throws out all that stuff Marco and I have so busily taught him: don't tease girls, don't touch girls if they say not to, don't hit people, solve things by talking about them. He throws all that out and when he gets to this far away nation or this village where everyone has dark skin or slanty eyes, he rapes the first woman he sees, then he hits her, or maybe he has to hit her first if she's not good. He shoots the first man he sees; he doesn't ask questions first. Or if he gets sent to some far off country where the people are already killing each other, and he doesn't forget everything we taught him but instead he picks up a child and spends five hours finding her mother, he rebuilds a road, or he gets two fighting leaders to sit down at the same table and leave their guns outside, someone back home on the Senate floor stands up and says, "Bring the boys back home. It's not in our national interest."

My friend Marcia comes over and brings her little boy. 49 He's six now and he takes one look at my giant belly and hides behind his mother. He's scared even though I've taped a dime over my belly button so it doesn't stick out. After we feed him ice cream though, he comes around. "When's your magic moment?" he says. When we laugh, he adds, "You know, when you get to hold it for the first time," as if he's speaking to a bunch of idiots.

Or if it's a girl—and we don't know if it's a boy or a girl, Marco didn't want to know—maybe if she's good, she'll get to be crossing guard at school. She'll play soccer and basketball and softball but she won't ever get to make money at it. Maybe if she's lucky she'll get a scholarship. Maybe she'll want to fly planes and even though we argue with her endlessly, she goes into the Navy and learns to sail jets off the decks of aircraft carriers. Despite everything, we're proud, but then her jet crashes and in the midst of all our grief—our baby girl is gone! her body never recovered from the sea—we have to listen to some old general on the news saying, "This just proves women can't fly planes." Maybe, instead, she'll be on the debate team in high school, and everyone will say she should be a lawyer. She can do that now pretty easily and maybe even get to make partner and make lots of money but then if she ever wants to have a baby of her own (and I WANT grandchildren) she'll have to quit or maybe if she's with a really enlightened firm, she won't have to quit and won't even have to come back to work full-time for a while, but at the least she'll hear whispering, "The men don't slack off like that when they have babies"—which is what happened to Marcia. She'll think that maybe they should, that maybe her husband should slack off at work—if she has a husband to father this baby—but if she knows what's good for her she'll keep her mouth shut.

On TV, thirteen white men faced off against Anita Hill. "Erotomania," they said. "Perjury," they said. "Have you ever read *The Exorcist*?" they asked. "It gets all tangled up in this sexual harassment crap," Simpson said. And Howell Heflin huffed and puffed his way through the hearings, waving that cigar around. Three years later, he pulled a pair of panties from his pocket during a press conference and laughed like it was some kind of prize. On TV we could watch the Gulf War in Technicolor—tracer missiles and smart bombs, F-16's, and Stealth Bombers. We're talking that weird green glow in the sky and lights like falling stars surrounded by haze. We're talking bombs hitting targets all marked out with circles and X's and then a splatter of electrons and the TV screen set up like a computer game. We're talking about the fact I can turn on CNN and see a war any day of the week: Bosnia, Rwanda, Haiti, Somalia, LA, Detroit, New York and Chechnya. And that's just for starters. I can turn it on and see body bags, dead bodies, body counts, and I can scream and scream for hours, as if those 13 white men and all the others could hear me. As if Newt could hear me, as if he'd stop in the middle of a speech about putting poor kids in orphanages and look up and maybe just pause to take a breath but definitely do something to show he'd heard me. As if they'd all—Jesse and Ollie and Ronald and George and George W. Bush the Third and Bob Dole and Michael Huffington with his millions—stop, look out of the set right at me and say, just like McNamara about Vietnam, "It's wrong. We were terribly wrong."

We're talking kids killing kids and fathers killing kids and mothers killing kids and fathers and mothers killing each other. "What's this world coming to!" my mother says. It drives her right out of the house and on to the porch where she's fanning herself with the newspaper. Maybe that's what I was aiming for, to get her out of the house—her with her good suggestions that I know are right, for writing calm and reasonable letters to my congressman, to my senators, her suggestions for doing volunteer work for Planned Parenthood or Habitat for Humanity ("I'm sure there's something you could do at home. Stuff envelopes or something," she says in exasperation). She snatches the newspaper right out of my hands now. "It doesn't need to upset you," she says. "Just stop worrying. It's none of your business anyway." How can she say that when I wake up in the morning to hear a whiny voice on the radio say, "It's like those people are double-dipping. You know, they get them food stamps and then the kids get that free lunch at school. I don't want my tax dollars goin for that"? How can she say it's none of my business when I wake up in the morning to hear a North Carolina legislator tell me women don't get pregnant when they're "really" raped? "None of the juices flow. It just doesn't happen," he says. When I wake up and hear that Newt divorced his wife, Jackie, when he first won election to Congress and she was diagnosed with cancer? When I hear that David Duke, one-time Grand Wizard of the Louisiana KKK, is running for governor again on the ticket that all people with AIDS should be tattooed in the genital area with glow-in-the-dark ink? I hear it and I want to throw up even though morning sickness hasn't bothered me for months. You see, if they're saying these things it means there are lots of people out there who believe them. After I've screamed myself out, my mother suggests I take some deep breaths and concentrate on knitting baby booties so this baby's tootsies won't get cold. Even she agrees it's a cold cold cold world out there—even though this baby's due any day now, in the heat of July. "No, not the Fourth of July," I said to the doctor. "I don't think I could take it," and I kept thinking red-white-and-blue, flags and patriotism, Veterans of Foreign Wars and Daughters of the American Revolution. I keep thinking how just up the street we wouldn't buy a house because the teeny tiny print at the end of the contract still said it couldn't be sold to black people. Well, that leaves Marco out. "Oh jeez, we don't go by that. It's just a relic," the real estate agent said but she also had no idea how to help us find the financing for that house. "Fraid so. Fourth of July's your due date," the doctor said. "Now, calm down, just calm down. Everything will be OK. You'll probably be late and get to go to the parade

51

anyway, but I'd suggest skipping the fireworks." And I think, "Shit. The fireworks. The only part of the Fourth that I like!"

It's afternoon and I've been yelling at the TV off and on for hours. They're holding hearings to cut funding for school lunches. They're holding hearings to find funding for another bomber. They're holding hearings on the nomination of Henry Foster to be Surgeon General, and Bob Dole says he won't let the nomination come to a vote on the Senate floor because Foster performed a perfectly legal procedure which happened to be an abortion. "Stop yelling," my mother says. "You can't do anything about any of this anyway." And I say, "Maybe that's why I'm yelling. Because they can't hear me. Because they won't hear me." I think, Little Baby, how can I love you so fiercely when I don't even know you? You're crammed in there, waiting, with your thumb in your mouth, your glassy slate-blue eyes closed, hiccupping. I'm so scared for you.

When Marco comes home at dusk, I scream at him that they're cutting the clean water act and I just heard on the news that one fifth of the cities in America already have substandard water. He says, "I know. I know. Those shits," he says. "What are we going to do?" he asks and he hugs me. I'm already thinking about letters to the editor, ads in *The New York Times* signed by every scientist in the country, but I take a break to open the bag he's brought home. He's brought us those red-white-and-blue rocket popsicles. We sit on the porch slurping on them, unsure if the world's going to blow up. The temperature's dropping to something bearable, and the sky's a limpid purple. On Tuesday night the fireworks will send up shocks of white and green and blue against that backdrop. Carol called the other day—they've followed up on an old lead and think it's probably algae that finally killed the birds. It's the same blue-green algae that blooms off-shore and makes shellfish inedible, perfectly natural, but how do you separate them? The bacteria and the chemicals that allow that algae to flourish, all the selenium from agricultural run-off that weakened the birds' immune systems? I think of the grebes doing their mating dance, the ones that are left, the way they seem to stand on the water and turn their heads from side to side, showing off their golden plumes. I think of their mellow voices, the koo-r-r-eep call across the lake, saying they're here, hoping for a reply.

WOMAN KILLS BROTHER'S LOVER IN FIT OF JEALOUS RAGE

I come to see you breech baby. You still my child, Ida, even in jail. Dark brown eyes, worry lines just starting to show in that sweet face, same brown sugar color as my Daddy and his Daddy before him, all those men I seen going off to work in the shipyards every morning, carrying they lunch in a sack. Ida, child, you look like you 'fraid I'm gonna slap you even though I never did, never slapped you or your brother even when I was hot and tired and you both screaming on the city bus. I yelled but I didn't slap. Your brother Kendall come into this world head first just like a baby suppose to, gave a little cry when his behind slapped, and never gave me no bother. Even now, he just sitting at home, quiet, reading a book or staring out the window or something. But then two years later, you come into the world ass first, head up near my heart, and ever since, Ida, you been doing these crazy wild ass things. One look from you and my milk dried up, had to feed you formula from a bottle. Then, when you one month old, you start crying, the same time every night. My girlfriend said, "May, that child gonna be trouble," but I said, "All babies cry. 'Sides, she got a good strong voice, know how to say what she want."

I know babies pull they mother's nose, tug on earrings till you think the flesh like to tear. Your brother Kendall did all that, but you different. You took Cream of Wheat cereal and rub it in my hair and I let you cause it kept you from doing worse. Three years old, you stuck out a little foot to trip me up, then you laughed and laughed, "Mama on the floor," but you laughed so hard I just had to laugh with you. When you seven or eight, you come home near every day without your underpants till I had to pin the waist elastic to the insides of your dresses.

Bet you think I don't remember but I remember it all, nothing I don't remember. Bet some this you don't even remember. I remember when you shaved your head, said it to show off the proud African shape of your skull, and I couldn't argue. It was fine—least once I got use to it. I guess I never told you that. You got yourself three earrings in one ear, a nose ring; I didn't ask where else you pierced. Some point you even took to carrying a gun—least I thought you did—but I just let you be, seem the best thing to do and 'sides, working two jobs, I was too tired to do much else. Finally all that craziness seem to pass. When you 'round seventeen, you start to straighten out, went to school, came right home. Have to admit I was happy with the change, 'cept you stopped talking too and I didn't like that. It didn't seem right you only saying, "Yes, Mama," or "No, Mama" when I axed you something. Then after you moved out, you start calling me up all hours confiding things, telling me jokes over the phone, and so I thought we got through all that silence too. Can't know how relieved I was. And now you go and do this, Ida. Why you need to do this? I keep looking at you just sitting there on the other side of the glass, and I keep axing myself that question.

Aunt Jerry told my cousin Lulu you filled with righteousness, doing the work of the Lord, but she always was crazy and she don't dare say it to my face. My girlfriends say you jealous, that why you done it. They say, "May, you let them sleep in the same bed when they kids?" And I say, "No. I didn't." And I didn't. You always had separate beds, little twin beds with matching quilts and stuffed animals with empty bellies to put pajamas in. Then when you ten and Kendall twelve, I moved into your room cause your Daddy gone by then anyway, and put him in my room that the double bed just filled up.

I caught him kissing another boy in there once, some scrawny boy from his class. Tongue kissing. Sitting on the bed cause there no where else to sit. I grab that other boy by the arm, pull him right up off that bed, and told him not to ever come back. When he gone, I said to your brother, "Don't you be doing that. I don't care if you practicing for the first time you kiss a girl. You suppose to be doing schoolwork, ain't you? Not that." When you come home, I could see you want to know why we just sitting around not talking, why he just sitting there with his arms all twist up over his chest, but you wouldn't axe, just went in the bedroom and shut the door. So now I'm telling you—since you always want to know so bad.

And remember that day last year you come by to show me that shiny blue suit you bought for your new job? I shoulda known right then there'd be trouble. You put that suit on in the bedroom and come out modeling it for me, axing, "How you like this Mama? Think Kendall'll like it?" Us finally giggling like girlfriends and me in the middle of saying how fine it make you look, when Kendall come home. He just come in and sit down at the table and we both turn to look at him, all dressed in black. "I went to another funeral today," he said. "I've been to six funerals in the last month. All my friends are dying, Mama."

"I'm your friend, ain't I? I ain't dead," you said. You had that pinched look your face always get when you eating something you don't like.

He didn't even look at you. He just kept looking at me, and even though he still my boy, I didn't say, "I'm so sorry, Son" or "That terrible" or "You make new friends. You good at that" or "You get through this terrible time with the help of the good Lord" or "We here for you. We your family." Instead, I said, "I got plenty friends died along the way too, and I ain't moping around." It just come out my mouth but I knew it a terrible thing to say, so I scooped out a big bowl of rice pudding I just took out the oven and put it down in front of him and said, "Eat that now. It good and sweet. Full of raisins." And he start to put one big spoon in his mouth after another without even blowing to cool them off, and the tears just running down his face. Meanwhile, I heard you go "Humph" and stomp into the bedroom in them new high heels and toss some things around and stomp out again, right out the door without even saying "Bye."

I shoulda known right then something wrong, but I didn't. I shoulda known back when you a little girl, showing off all the time for your big brother, doing cartwheels and twirly-twirls so your skirt puff up. I shoulda known when I seen you could just watch him for hours. He'd be watching cartoons on the TV, and you'd be watching him, staring like. Then that time I come by the school and you mouthing off to some them bigger kids, fists up, and Kendall tugging your sleeve, saying,

55

"Ida, come on. Come on. Let's go." I shoulda known right then you gonna be nothing by trouble just like my girlfriends said, but I didn't; I thought you being tough and brave. Just last week when you axed me, "You heard from Kendall, Mama? What's going on with him? I never see him. Don't he like me no more?" I shoulda known something wrong, but I just laughed and told you I ain't seen him for a while either.

You weren't around last summer when he told me he was in love. Or he didn't tell me but I knew cause he kept talking about this person, giving him a girl name—Tammy—even though I 'spected it had to be a boy. And every time he talked about him—T. do this; T. do that—he turn coppery, all the blood up in his face, just the color of a set of fancy wood furniture your Daddy and I was set on buying once. And I thought, This is sure a big love. This the one make him think there an army of ants crawling up his back, all the way up from his behind to his shoulders, and when they get to the top, they start over again. This the one make him shake so hard when he talk to him, he got to clench his teeth so his heart don't get shook right up out his mouth. Then I seen them together, right on the corner of Market and Powell—my boy and this big blond man standing over him. Hair like white ash, wearing some those tight leather pants and a tank top that show off his muscles, even though it summer in San Francisco and no weather for baring skin. I thought, "Had to be a man, couldn't he least pick a black man!" and I started to turn away. Then Kendall seen me and touched Ted on the arm and led him over. "Mama, this is Ted," he said, and he seem so happy, I just had to stretch out my hand to shake. I couldn't stay mad. "Please to meet you. I think I heard a lot about you. Very please to meet you," I said and I was cause Ted was smiling like he just real happy to be standing right there with Kendall and me, not a trouble in the world, and cause his eyes was the color of huckleberries though I know that ain't possible—musta been the light—and cause after we said our good-byes and they turn to cross the street, he put his big hand right at the small of my boy's back like he protecting something precious.

You see, baby, people love who they love, no explanation. That just the way it is. I wonder how you don't know that. You just sitting there in that bright orange suit they give everybody to wear in jail. Orange ain't never been your color but you don't seem to care. You just looking at your hands

56

like the blood still on them. Like you still thinking about walking down the street last week, and deciding to go on up to your brother's place. Like you thinking about pushing on the door when no one answer, thinking it funny it open, thinking he must be on the phone. Like you still thinking about finding them with no clothes on, naked brother and that big white man on the bed with him. Like you thinking about running up to them like a child run up to her Mama and Daddy caught making love when she come home early from school, not stopping to play, running to show her Mama all A's on her report card. Like you still thinking it must hurt, one person hurting the other—that what the moaning all about—but you got to know that ain't so by now. You got to, don't you? I always thought you just secretive, some children are—just secretive about the ones they love. They don't ask questions or tell stories. So I always thought you like that but maybe that ain't so. Maybe you never had nothing to be secretive about. Maybe there gaps in you I don't know nothing about, and that make me even sadder than before.

I'm thinking about your brother, sitting in my place all stiff like somebody slapped him. I think how he didn't say nothing when I told him, "I liked him that one time I met him. I wish I'd got to know him more." I'm thinking how he ain't said nothing for seven days now, not one word. They say he in shock so's he can't even tell them is the knife from his own kitchen or not.

Oh Ida, I don't know if you done this cause Ted white, cause he a man, or cause he anybody but you. Any reason, it wrong. But I still love you, Ida. You still my baby girl, even in here. I want to say it but we both just sitting here looking at your hands, and I can't tell what you thinking—just like when you a baby crying every night and nothing I did could make you stop. Breech baby, I sigh when the guard say it time to go. Wild thing. "I come to see you tomorrow. I bring you a pretty ribbon to put in your hair if they let me, and a piece of banana cake."

57

INTERROGATING THE VOICE

Why did this voice come to me? And once it did, should I have taken it on? Am I stealing something? Or am I exercising the writer's right to write beyond autobiography? Everyone's right—the right to the imagination? I could make an argument for freedom here, present a list of carefully considered reasons why a writer might choose to invent a voice so clearly different from her own, but the way this story came to me was any way but free. I did not choose this voice. It chose me.

I woke at 3 a.m. and she was by my ear, saying, "Breech baby," talking the whole story to me as if I were her daughter. Whether my story has captured her voice successfully or not, I knew she was black, in her 40's, working class. There was simply no doubt about it. She spoke to me as if she, an actual person, had snuck into the house and crept to my bedside in the dark, just the way I've heard other writers say the voices of characters come to them—magically, unbidden. I'd always laughed at this idea—too mystical, too irrational—and here it was, happening to me, a voice knocking on the brain's door, demanding to be let in, intent on telling its story, and because I was in bed and the apartment was cold and dark, I started speaking her story in a whisper, her voice coming through me now—mouth, teeth, tongue—daughter become mother. Through the night, I repeated the story so I'd be certain not to forget it, and in the morning, even before making coffee, I sat myself down and wrote, a stream of words from the end of the pen.

There. I've gone and Romanticized the process. Given myself a muse, even if she's not the traditional blond sylph. I've made it seem inevitable and necessary that I write this story down, just as I heard it, the words flowing into my ear and out my fingers, smoothly, purely. Well, not quite so purely perhaps.

"Capture." I used that word automatically. We like to think the word means "is true to" or "recreates accurately" but stop, think about more workaday meanings: taken against one's will, violence, pain, entrapment, not allowed to speak, stolen. We're back to the idea of freedom—and lack of freedom. Not now a question of the writer captive to a muse or to autobiography but the writer as captor. In my midnight story, have I implicated myself, just another writer plundering whatever riches she finds? Just another privileged thief? And now, here, in my daytime essay, am I trying to plea bargain, or even to deny the guilt?

I tried to rewrite this story white, making the lover a black man—but it was the voice I loved here, the music of it, the rise and fall. Yes, I loved it; I wanted to keep hearing it and hearing it. That's why, half-asleep, I repeated May's story. That's why, all summer, I kept reading and reading more and going to readings — Toni Morrison and Toni Cade Bambara and Gloria Naylor and Wanda Coleman and Paule Marshall and Becky Birtha and Xam Cartier and Ntozake Shange, Jess Mowry and Terri McMillan. Wanda Coleman stood on stage and everything about her was imposing — voice and body and mind. Beside her, she had a suitcase propped open, a suitcase completely full of poems, and as she chanted her way through all those poems, I thought, "Yes, I am trying to steal power." An odd sort of power, a music that comes from trouble: no — from contending with trouble. Because, also, all summer, I rode the bus to work, from Fifty-first Street down Broadway to City Center. I didn't need to be there until mid-morning, outside the regular commute hours, when only poor people rode the bus, and in that part of Oakland, that mostly meant black people. Every morning I heard mothers scold their kids, ready to slap or grab an arm with the rough hand of love, take a deep breath and start to explain or shout. I heard lovers exchange whispers, assure each other how it would all be all right, as they helped each other down the steps in front of the Kaiser hospital at the corner of MacArthur, right there where the gold Christmas decorations go up on the mall every year, and every year more stores close, where not too long ago, some guy got shot for bumping into some other guy's girl. At lunch time, I read William Labov's *Language in the Inner City: Studies in the Black English Vernacular*; I made lists and lists of characteristics; I read about the way the future tense is used and the past, the copula and the possessive. I read *Black Talk: Words and Phrases from the Hood to the Amen Corner, Talkin and Testifyin, Them Children: A Study in Language Learning,* and *Third Ear: A Black Glossary*. I took a lexicon of Black English out of the library and carried it around, heavy in the straw bag that also held my lunch, sun block, house keys, and spare toothbrush. Every day, after work, I took the bus into West Oakland. I rode it around the big postal depot and the train yards, rigged with a tape recorder. I was looking for her, I guess, among the women who came off the shift at the Nabisco Plant, wearing hairnets, blue uniforms, and spongy white shoes; carrying sacks of day-old cookies; and smelling sweet like bread. I sat where they couldn't see me and listened as

59

they traded recipes for turkey necks, talked about husbands who worked days at the post office so they hardly got to see each other, worried aloud about their kids — the older boy who was good at baseball and the younger one who was a whiz at math but having trouble learning to read. Then when I got home, I listened to the tapes, sitting in the dark and tuning out the sirens and the hiss of bus wheels so I could hear the voices again. I wanted to keep hearing them and hearing them.

I guess that's why I wrote down May's story. I loved the voice, even as I asked myself where my own grandmother was, why she hadn't come to me in the middle of the night, whispering to me, speaking through me. Her voice, the memory of her voice, is certainly musical, her Yiddish-inflected English — questions answered with questions, insults that stagger the imagination (may you grow like an onion with your head in the ground and your feet always in the air), the dark humor. Why didn't I invoke her ghost? I have a photo of her climbing a hill, lugging a pail, and her face is full of sixty years of trouble. I think how she came all alone from Russia at the age of twelve; worked as seamstress, baker, nurse's aid; married a man who was much older than herself who then took up with one younger woman after another until she wondered whether the women in the old country, their men bent over the Talmud, had something going for them after all, until she finally said enough is enough; brought up four children, alternately whipping and praising; rose in the dark to hand out union leaflets at factory gates; protested against injustice and war nearly until her death. I have some jewelry of hers — a purple cut glass pin shaped like a flower, a monstrous growth that, when I wear it, pulls dress fabric askew. She was larger than life too, I think, powerful, and then with a laugh, I remember her strapping herself into one of those horrible, pink, armor-like corsets old ladies wore — built-in bra, girdle, and garters. And even with this detail, the fleshy pink corset and the white fleshier flesh of her upper arms and thighs and the jiggling tops of her breasts, the detail that's supposed to make the character come alive, I still don't know why, that night, her voice was completely silent and I fell in love with the voice of Ida and Kendall's mother, with May's voice. I just don't know.

A year and a half later, I'm still stumbling around all these questions. I think I may be in the middle of a mystery, something inscrutable about inspiration. Are there several women here facing each other across time, space, race? The imagination a bridge? Or just one crazed woman searching for a sound she wants to take for her own? In my most hopeful moments, I imagine my grandmother and May sitting across from each other on a city bus, eyeing each other, then speaking. It turns out they know some of the same things: how to raise children against adversity, for example. Inside, I still hear two voices, not their voices but two of my own, irreconcilable. One says forget this sorry explanation; you're whining. Just tell the story. This voice keeps me going—on to the next word, page, project. But the other voice won't stop whispering, tentative and doubtful. This second voice questions constantly: is this right? is this good enough? I suspect it's suicide not to question, and so I try to prop this voice up, borrow bravery from the first voice—not chin-up, stiff-upper-lip bravery but something else—and acknowledge there is, finally, no explanation for love.

ABSINTHE

Paris? I'm still here. It was spring when we got here. It's winter now. OK, so it's colder, but the gray days still run into each other like they did the whole time. I get up in the morning, go out for a smoke and some coffee. Later maybe I take a walk around the neighborhood, stop in some place and have a beer and then another. Outside there's dirty water rushing through the gutters. Then someone comes along and moves the balled up rag that blocks it so now it goes a different way. That's his job. To move rags around in the streets. I guess I'm waiting for the money to run out. I'm waiting for I don't know what. I'm waiting for it to sink in that she's gone.

When we got here, Ella's hair was long. She had to keep shoving it out of the way when she went to get the cases at the baggage claim—mine, hers, Dave's, Rick's, Charlie's, drums and guitars and amps. We got the van and drove into the city through some crazy traffic. We must of hit rush hour. Like in any American city but I just sat and watched. Paris didn't look like a map or a postcard picture taken from the top of some building where you can see the avenues and monuments and neighborhoods all spread out. You couldn't see any landmarks at all. Instead you saw one big concrete apartment building after another. One train yard after another. Gray walls with these old posters peeling off them. "The banlieu," Ella said. "These are the suburbs." We got lost on the road that goes round the city. There're supposed to be exits off it that lead you down big wide streets right into the center of town but we kept missing the one we wanted. "Fuck it. Just take another one," Charlie said, but Dave was driving and he said, "No man, we'll get lost." So we drove round and round in circles until Rick said, "Louie, you got the map. Which way should we go?" but I didn't care. I just kept watching until it all looked the same—city, road, city, road. We went round the city maybe twelve times. Ella'd tell you in French. She'd say, "Wee. A doo-zen fwa." She can speak French. Could speak French. No, can speak French—just not here, just not around me. That's right, I have to keep telling myself, you shit, she's gone. For a sec it's like being pricked by a pin: all that stuff is past. Remember you came back and everything of hers was gone? Remember what it looked like? Remember? Empty. Remember that.

Paris? It's winter so most of the day is night. At nine-thirty the streetlights get turned off. I got up early one day cause I couldn't sleep—nine or something—and it was still dark out. Can you believe it? Nine in the fucking morning. Even when it does start to get light, the clouds don't go away. Most of the buildings are dark too—that's what I notice when I walk around. It's dark and wet. Those gargoyles sit up there and spit on you. At three-thirty when I'm sitting here having a beer, the lamps get turned on again. In an hour, it's like the street turns into some sort of a play. I can see everybody going around into the different lighted stores. They go to the boulangerie and the charcuterie and the vegetable stand. Then they stop off in the café here for their pernods and their glasses of wine. They talk this real fast French I thought I was getting to understand, but their mouths move like behind a screen. You're supposed to think these people've known each other for a really long time and are so happy to see each other— they do that three kisses on alternating cheeks thing. I don't believe it though. I don't believe anything since Ella's gone. Yesterday I ran into this guy I know from Les Mouches. I ran right into him and he said, "Pardon," but I could tell he didn't know who I was. We played together just three weeks ago but it was like he was looking at a fish or something.

I walked in the place that day and everything was gone 'cept the bare furniture that was there when we moved in. My stuff was sort of thrown around—dirty clothes and notebooks and guitar cases and shit—but all her stuff was gone. I keep seeing it. I keep turning the key. I open the door and walk into the place and see that something's wrong and figure it out all over again, like I'm playing some movie scene over and over in my head. I'm watching it and in it at the

63

same time but I'm totally far away from it all too. And then I stop thinking about it and she's still here. And sometimes I'm walking around and I catch myself talking to her, you know, lips moving and everything, but I think, "Well, who cares anyway." Also, there hasn't been any music in my head. I mean, there always used to be music in my head. And when there is music now, it's these sappy old songs—"Cold Cold Heart" or some shit that my Grandma used to listen to. It's playing and playing. I can't make it stop. I just say, "Ella, come on, stop it, turn it off." I'm just walking and my steps don't follow any beat, just One One One One One one after the other. Each foot is heavy.

CITY OF LIGHT

When I come home, there's a square of cardboard under the door. It says, "MONSIEUR ASIYA: Man of God and Great Seer, hereditary gift from father to son." My French is good enough so I can make it out OK. "Specialist in problems of love, work, luck. Absolute fidelity between man and wife. Mysterious illnesses. Sterility. If your spouse has left, he or she will return during the same week. Nightmares. Crises." It has a phone number I can call. There's an address where I can drop by—24 hours a day, it says. It's right around the corner. I should do this, I think, but I just sit down and stare at it. He could bring her back. Or if she's already dead somewhere, he could contact her and I could talk to her. Her voice'll cut sweet, like she's still here.

When we got here, we got off the plane and it was light already, sort of a hazy blue everywhere. We flew all night. The whole time Ella had her head on my shoulder like some big planet. I didn't sleep. I was that wound up. It meant when we landed I was running on that wired acid up-all-night energy. So were the other guys. But Ella, she was calm.

Ella—the first time she comes into the bar where we're playing, and I see her from the stage as we go into "6th Street Bash." The light hits her head just right and her hair looks like white bristle next to her skull. My heart jumps right up into my eyes. She hangs out after the set is over. Sort of off to the side like she's waiting for someone. We're waiting to split up the money with the other band and flicking cigarette butts

across the room and watching the lit orange ends whiz over
into the blue light near the stage. They fall and sizzle behind
a table. She comes right up to me and says she can spit that
far. I bet her she can't but she does. Then she takes her big
black-framed glasses off to rub her eyes. I see her flimsy skull
and her neck bent right over and the tattoo of a horse. And
her white white skin you can see the veins through. They're
blue and then green after I draw over them with magic marker.
We go to my place and knot up the sheets. After, she lays
there on the bed with no clothes on. I get out the jar with the
markers—some spill under the bed, rolling around in the
dirt—cuz she's just laying there with her hands under her
head, staring at the ceiling and not talking to me. I take one
and draw all over around her nipple until her left tit looks
like a bloodshot eye. She just smiles. Doesn't laugh. Doesn't
tell me Stop. Doesn't push my hand away. "Not ticklish, huh?"
I say. "Nope," she says. She must like the way it feels. I draw
up the inside of my arm with the purple one and it gives me a
chill. When it dries, it feels like someone stitched thread
through the skin and pulled the end. We spend all night laying
there. We screw again and again. She always wants to.

When she leaves in the morning, I see she has this big
stack of books. I say, "I'll take 'em to your car." She says,
"Fuck off. I don't have a car and I bet I'm stronger than you
anyway. All you do is sing and drink." "I do some other things
OK too, don't I?" I say and she laughs. She puts the books
down and starts telling me about them. They're all falling
apart. I turn some pages. The paper is crinkly like the
cellophane on cigarette packs and they're all in a language I
can't read. "You probably can't read any language," she laughs
at me. But she's staring at me with eyes the color of Mentho-
Lyptus. They're eyes that won't go away. Then she makes me
read and says, "OK, I guess you can be my boyfriend." She's
still looking at me. "Deal," I say, "but no reading when I'm
around." "Don't worry," she says, "there are better things to
do when you're around. And I can read with other people.
Just don't get mad when I do." I tell her I like to read too. I
read on the bus when we're driving from one gig to another if
I can keep myself from getting sick.

The phone rings and it's Charlie calling from New York.
They went back for Christmas which is nothing here anyway.
There aren't any decorations up and it seems like everybody

65

leaves town or maybe they hole up with their Grandmamas and eat big meals and go to church. All the clubs close and then on New Year's they bring in some big name band to play. "You should come back here," he says.

"I should?" I say. "I don't know."

"So are you saying you're not coming back?"

"No," I say. "I'm not saying that. I'm not saying anything like that. I just don't know."

"What are you saying, Louie?"

I say, "I thought you guys were coming back <u>here</u>. All your stuff's here."

"Look," Charlie says, "we got to know when you're coming back cuz things're happening here. I mean things could happen. Izzy heard those demos we brought back. I'm calling from his place now. He thinks he can get us a contract, money for a video and everything. But, man, they're all your songs. You got to come back."

I stand with the phone getting hot in my hand. I'm thinking how this could really be a big break. I'm thinking how he's right. They <u>are</u> all my songs but I don't remember writing them. When did I write them? "I can't leave," I say. "What about Ella?"

"What about her? Just tell her you need to go to the States. She should be happy for us anyway."

"She's gone. I don't know where she is."

"Well find her then. Where is she? At the library or something?"

"No, man, I don't know."

"What d'you mean, you don't know? You know all the places she hangs out."

I think, Yeah, I know all the places she hangs out. She's probably at the library or something. "I'll call you back," I say, and before he can say anything, I hang up and grab my coat and head out the door. I'll go to her favorite café first, that one by the Seine.

I pass by the bread store and wave to the lady there because I'm going to find Ella. She's going to be sitting there, right where she always sits to smoke and have a kir on her way home. She's going to be sitting there and looking at the river. The first day we got here we walked this way, right through this alley. By the time we got the van unloaded, we heard rumbling. Thunder. Ella was standing in the doorway

and looking up at a sky full of big black clouds. I went over
and put my arm around her. "Some April in Paris, huh?" I
said. "Let's go watch the lightning over the Seine," she said.
She twisted her hair up and tied it around itself. It's dyed
black now and long long like some hippie chick from the
sixties. Like some girl who would of hung out with the
Grateful Dead or the Jefferson Airplane instead of with us but
I like it anyway.

The others say they want to get some shut eye, so we leave
them and go out. I'm tired too but I'm not gonna go to sleep
when we just got here, not when Ella's pulling me by the arm.
Outside there's a courtyard with a few dead trees in tubs and
people's wet clothes hanging from their windows. It's real
quiet, like everyone is hiding. Like they're all scared of storms.
We're not scared of storms. Out on the street, the metal shutters
are still pulled down over all the store windows. On the corner
there's a café with orange plastic chairs on the sidewalk and
no one sitting in them. I can see Ella and me going there every
morning for coffee. I pick out the table where we're gonna
(where we did? No, where we're gonna) sit and watch people.
There are maybe one or two old dames walking by, taking
their dogs out for a piss and talking to them all sweet, telling
them how they're going to go home now and have some nice
dinner. It's kind of cute. Even I can understand what they're
saying to their dogs.

Ella's up at the next corner. She turns around to see where
I am and waves. When I get there, she takes my hand. We
walk and walk and walk. We turn corners right and left cuz
Ella knows where we're going. "This is Bastille," she says. I
see a green column topped by a winged man painted gold.
"Where's the prison?" I ask. "Isn't there supposed to be a prison
here?" "Not for a couple hundred years," she says.

We walk until we come to the river. I keep humming,
trying to remember some song. The whole time the sky's
rumbling and the clouds are shouting and threatening but it
doesn't rain. The river looks green. The color of a marble.
We run like crazy down some ramps. I think Ella's gonna trip
and break her teeth so I grab her shirt. Then I grab her arm
and we run the rest of the way like that, together. At the
bottom, I kiss her hard on the mouth, feel her tongue like the
muscle it is, her breasts pressed against me until we see the
old guys hanging out under the bridge. I yell, "Hey come out.

It's not gonna rain." But Ella says, "They don't understand you. They probably think you're being mean." Her eyes tease. "So translate for me," I say, and she does, but the old guys just laugh and stay where they are and pass a bottle around in a brown paper bag, just like hobos at home, hobos anywhere. The water down here's more gray than green, more brown than gray, but on top specks of white stuff like soapsuds keep making pretty patterns. Then the lightning comes and turns everything the blue negative of itself but just for one second and it doesn't rain. Ella gets up behind me and puts her arms around my waist. Her arms are solid and hard and she links her fingers together over my stomach.

And now I'm here at the Seine and looking for Ella and the café is lit up the sulfur yellow of a match and even from outside I can tell it's empty. She's not here reading *Le Monde*. The same couple isn't sitting near the window as always, holding hands and drinking chocolat chaud with extra sugar. Ella isn't reading to me out of the newspaper. "You're not listening," Ella doesn't say in French and then in English when I don't answer.

"Have you seen Ella?" I ask the guy at the bar. I know he knows her. He's talked to us together lots of times. "Ah, non," he tells me, "not for two weeks," and shrugs his shoulders and sticks out his chin like the French always do when they don't know something but think they should. If she's not here it means she found another café she likes better or she's already on her way home. I rush out because I remember there's something I need to tell her. I need to tell her that I need to go to New York because we're getting our big break. I need to tell her that all her work paid off, all those times she yelled at us to practice, all that work she did booking us into the clubs here and finding us the studio to record the demo and sitting there with us until it was done and making sure it sounded just right. I need to tell her that. She'll be so happy. I'm racing home and this bass line starts going through my head, just this bass line, in time to my feet: dum da, dum da, dum dee dee dum da. Something real simple, and I can't stop thinking it as I'm walking. I'm thinking how Rick's gonna beat it to hell and Dave's gonna get it to grow and Charlie's gonna make his guitar wind around it like a great big fucking wave.

I'm thinking how most bands go to England to make it but we came to Paris. They liked us here and, besides, Ella speaks French so she can translate for us and be our manager and she has money from school to pay most of the rent. She's here anyway looking stuff up for her final PhD paper so she can go out and get a job somewhere. I joked that then she could support me and when we go back to the States I won't have to have a day job, but I didn't mean it. I wouldn't let her do it. And now I won't need to at all. It's all worked out, I'll tell her. It was all worth it. I'll remind her how the band started playing these clubs down in basements here in the worst parts of town. Just like clubs like that always are, all over the world. There's a little room in back where we can sit before we play but we have to go out front and through all the people to get to the john. People just cram up front or stand on chairs or on the tables. Like that time me and Ella went to see Sonic Youth and we just walked table to table up to the front of the room. If you turn on the late night video show here, you might think all anybody likes are accordion bands but it's not true. Every time we saw some kid with scruffy shoes and jeans that didn't look clean, we gave them a flyer. It must of worked cuz by June we were playing every weekend and a couple other nights a week too. All those kids came and students sort of plastered against the walls to stay safe and people old enough to have bought the first Ramones record when it was new. So many people. Better than New York. The place so fucking hot the sweat just poured off everybody and it all mixed together. People climbed up on stage to jump off. They sailed and the crowd caught them. People climbed up on stage and just stayed there. They wouldn't go away even when we pushed them.

69

We did "Break It Up" and then that X song "We're Having Much More Fun," but we do it dark, really dark, even darker than X ever did it and really really fast. Once this old guy with a long beard came up to me at one of our shows and said, "Yeah, man, thanks for coming," but I just thought, "Fuck it. Not the way we play. If your heart beat that fast you'd probably be fucking dead." And Ella's standing off to the side, out of the way of the flying bodies. I turn to the guitar and the feedback squeal, the wail when you bend over it right up at the amp, and the strut-thump-flutter when you flap both hands against the strings. It goes ringing and Rick and Dave play off each other, play off that big steady beat on drums and bass, wall of noise and some melody just skulks inside.

And then it explodes, it explodes. Then it all explodes. Ella's right up close to the stage. She's flung back. She's smiling.

One night we get our money and pack up and get in the van. We're all beat. There's a tape playing in the deck—Black Flag and Circle Jerks and Avengers, old stuff but good. I'm sitting there in the front seat with my eyes half-closed and Ella on my lap cuz there's no where else for her to sit. I take the money out of her shirt pocket. "Thanks babe," I say. "We couldn't do this without you." "Yeah you could," she says. "You're right. We could," I say. Then I whisper in her ear, "But I wouldn't want to," and she kisses me.

We start driving and Rick turns around and looks out the back window. He says, "Hey look, the Eiffel Tower's all lit up," like he's never seen it before. "Let's go there. Let's go to the top right now." Ella says, "You can't get up there at night. It's closed." But Dave stops the van and we all climb on top of it to look. We can see the whole city lined out in white like some neon drug. You know how it is. It looks like a fairy map. It looks like the best pinball machine in the world. I whisper, "Isn't it pretty?" into Ella's ear.

70

"Isn't it pretty? Isn't it pretty?" I realize I'm whispering it even now when I'm walking up our street. All the shops are closing. I should pick up something to eat, I think, but then I think if Ella's home she might want to go out so I just keep walking. That bass line starts going through my head again, and I think, "I've got this girl/Best girl, best girl/Best girl in the world" and there's a tune to it. Then I think, No, "I love this girl/Hard, hard, hard but the best girl in the world." I don't write love songs but I can't get it out of my head so I keep singing it all the way home. I think we could shout that. We could shout it, then we could whisper it. I could work up some verses all about Ella. This afternoon, I found one thing she left, her razor in the shower. I almost threw it out but what if she wants it? She'll need to know just where to find it. So I left it there. I put it back down. I'm not going to touch it.

Walking with Ella's like floating. It's like being just high enough before you start to nod. It's like having four drinks, not five. It's like the world's just starting to go sideways. The sky glows. We're in Monceau Park and Ella says the broken columns and fake statues make it seem like we're in Rome, like we're looking at old ruins. We've traveled back in time.

"Let's go to Rome," I say. "We can go tonight. Just me and you." In the middle of the park, we spin each other around so fast we get dizzy. We have to hold each other up. It's spring and the air is clear. It's bright. Sun and flower petals fall out of the blue sky. There are flowers up in the trees and that's very weird but beautiful. I can see every baby leaf up there in its clear green blanket.

At home the lights're on but she's not there. She must have been here and gone out again, I think, and I feel like kicking myself for not leaving her a note. I should have said, "Wait for me. Do NOT go anywhere without me. I'll be back soon." When she doesn't come back by midnight, I start calling her friends, the ones she sits with in the library—I see them when I go to pick her up. Maybe she's staying with one of them cuz it got late. They all stay up late so they don't care that I'm calling, but they don't know where she is. Finally I ask, "What about those out of town libraries? Think she went to one of those for a few days? She's always talking about how she had to go look things up in those." But they say that, no, those are all closed for the holidays too, but I think, Jesus, one them somewhere has to be open. Then I think maybe Ella told me she was going home for the holidays and I just forgot even though that would be really stupid. But when I call New Jersey it's six at night and her mother's getting ready to go out to a party. It's clear Ella's not there so I pretend I'm just calling to say Merry Christmas, and then I just sit and sit and wait and fall asleep in the chair.

    For a couple days I wander around looking for her. I go to the library but it's closed. I go to her favorite restaurant and I have lunch, waiting for her, but she doesn't show up. In the morning, I wake up and hear her putting on her long coat and beret and long leather gloves and locking the door behind her. At night I hear her footsteps on the tiles in the hall, the clickety-click of those new shoes she bought, the ones with high heels that make her almost as tall as me. I see her little toes crushed into the ends of those pointy shoes, I see how she stretches them and curls them when she takes her shoes off, but she turns in at a different door and by the time I get to our peephole, I can't even see which one it was. One day I just see her, on the metro platform, her long black hair and the back of her black coat, but the train comes and the gates swing closed and I can't reach her. Then the next day I see her twice, and then more and more. I see her at the market buying shrimp with the heads still on (best girl, best girl), and I see her looking through prints at the bouquinistes along the quais (best girl). I know it's her because she likes to do that, even in the rain like today, even though she's got a new short haircut, sort of a bob, and she's wearting a little suit and a raincoat over it. Still, I know it's her because it's her way of standing until I see she's got a Hermes scarf, one of those ones with horses all over it and then I change my mind. It can't be her. She'd never wear one of those. She's always making fun of the old ladies who wear them.

When Charlie calls in the morning he wakes me up and he's mad since I never called him back. I even sort of forgot I was supposed to because I've been looking so hard for Ella. "She's still gone?" he says. "What? Is she out of town or something?" When I tell him I don't really know but I'm getting closer to finding her every day, he says, "Jesus, Louie, she's not worth it. Leave her a note or something and get on a plane. You're gonna blow this chance we have," but I finally convince him that it's OK if I stay here until after New Year's, that nothing'll happen before then. "She'll be back by then and I can explain everything. Besides, then she can help me box up all this shit you guys left for me to deal with."

"Sorry about that, man," Charlie says. "How could we know things would be breaking here?"

I go out to get something to eat, chocolate bars and milk and cereal at Ed's and see women there stuffing their carts with more than one person can possibly eat. On the way home I pass by the laundry where some guy's folding panties into tiny packages. At home, there's another square of cardboard under the door. This one says, "MADAME DORA – palm reader, tarots. Secret for finding lost loves. You who have tried everything, you who no longer believe in anything, I offer you luck and happiness in all spheres by the gifts and powers transmitted to me from my ancestors. Very human, I will help you to conquer fatality." I think how it's two in the afternoon and I haven't seen Ella once today yet so I check out Madame Dora's address, somewhere up hear Gare du Nord and that big boulevard where all the really cheap clothing stores are. Her place is through a courtyard filled with trash cans and up some stairs. She's a tiny woman in slippers and one of those flowered housedresses Paris housewives wear, like I've taken her away from scrubbing the floors. She looks real tired but she can see me, she says, she can help me. "What is it about?" she asks. "What do you want to know? About your future, yes?"

"Une fille," I say. "Mon amie. Ma fiancée. I know you can help me find her."

She stares at me and she doesn't ask me into the dining room where I can see a table set up with a red cloth over it and a huge deck of cards and even a crystal ball. She takes my hand but she doesn't look at my palm. She just stares at me a long long time. Finally she puts her hand on my forehead and says, "Pauvre petit," even though she has to reach way up to touch me. "Il n'y a pas de fille."

PASSAGE DU DRAGON

In the morning I think how Ella never loved me. I'm making coffee in one of these stupid little pots they have here when you can only make one cup at a time. I slam it down and the coffee grounds fly everywhere. She thought it was cool or something to be with a guy in a band but she never loved me. If she was really out of town looking things up in libraries she'd be back by now or she would at least have called. She never thought this could work. Any of it.

73

I sit down with the coffee and a hunk of stale bread—it goes stale in one day here—and I think how right after we got here, she said, "The French are different you know. They're into a whole different kind of music. They like really poppy American songs and weepy cabaret singers, Edith Piaf, stuff like that." Right after we got here and she was already saying shit like that.

"Come on, Ella," I said. "Music's the fucking universal language. You know that. There have to be some people here who like loud music instead of that wimpy shit."

"I don't know," she said. At first I thought she was laughing. We were just sitting here drinking coffee then too, but she wasn't laughing. "When they decide to be rebellious here, they go all out and have a revolution. They're not into just pretending to have little mini-rebellions every day by listening to a certain type of music."

"Aw, come on, Ella. Besides, who gives a shit if only a few hundred people like us. As long as we get to keep playing. It's our music. We're gonna play what we want."

"Hey guys, let's go out for a beer," Dave said. He must of come up behind me, but we both ignored him.

Ella got up and stood by the kitchen door. She gave me her you're-so-stupid look, where she sighs and looks down and pinches the top of her nose. "I'm just warning you so you're not disappointed," she said. "Don't be disappointed if you don't get big crowds. Don't be disappointed if the kids who come don't look like you expect."

"Don't tell me what to expect," I said right in her face. "What is this shit anyway? You were pretty keen on this before."

"OK. OK," Ella said. "I just don't want you to be disappointed."

When I turned around, the guys were gone. They'd gone out for that beer without us, and I chased after them. I thought I'd gotten to her, but she didn't believe me. She was just pretending.

Later, the one time I slapped her, she asked for it. "Your playing's getting sloppy," she kept saying. Her cheek turned red, and her hand went up to it. Then she hit me back. "Hey," I said.

Why didn't this happen to one of the other guys anyway? Rick was always screwing around. He always had something on the side, but he dropped <u>them</u>, not the other way round. And the whole time his girlfriend back in New York kept writing to him, sending him presents and shit. It should have been him, not me. He should have gotten back to his place on Avenue A and found the locks changes. But that's not what happened. Charlie said she met them at the airport and then practically fucked him in the back of the cab on the way into the city. I should have done what he did. It wouldn't have mattered anyway.

One day in the summer, we were walking around the center of town — me, him and Ella, I don't remember what for — and it was so hot the girls weren't wearing any stockings. Ella pointed it out. They wore suits with short sleeves and short tight tight tight skirts, and real high heels, but no stockings. They looked like they should be wearing stockings. They looked like they worked in offices. Like they answered phones or kept the books or figured out just how the pages of a magazine should look. Their hips twitched and they trotted down the street like they were definitely going somewhere. They wore real red lipstick, dark and hard, no fairy pink like little girls in the States or even Moms taking their kids to the mall. We were sitting in a café on a narrow street, just killing time—the apartment was too hot—and I saw their mouths left red marks on everything. They crossed their legs at the café tables and I thought I could get down and lick the sweat off their skin. I could slide my hand right up and down their legs, right on skin, all the way up the inside of their thighs. I wanted to but I didn't do it.

Rick started to get up to follow girls and yelling ooh-la-la really loud. He'd follow a girl a few steps and then sit back down, but he followed this one girl until she turned around and gave him a faceful of French so fast you would have thought it was all one word. He stood there looking stupid, but then he said, "Cool it, babe. Cool it." Me and Ella watched from back at the café. We laughed and laughed but she wouldn't tell me what the French girl was saying. I said, "I bet she's saying 'It's too hot for this shit. Get outta my face.' That's what you would say." But Ella said you just couldn't translate it. It wouldn't make any sense in English. It wouldn't even sound like an insult. So I said, "So what should I say so they won't fucking yell at me?" She said, "You want me to tell you how to pick up French girls? Are you kidding? I'm not telling you that." And I didn't really mean it anyway cuz it was this crazy thing by then of me not wanting anyone else. The stupid bitch. I loved her <u>that</u> much. I pulled her over and she sat in my lap. Ella—she was wearing a black T-shirt with a hole in the shoulder I stuck my finger in. Through it her skin felt cool. I loved her and she wouldn't even wear the jewelry I gave her. It was a silver ring I picked up on St. Mark's of two snakes twisted up. I teased her she was afraid someone'd cut it off her hand in the Metro. I said, "This isn't New York. No one's gonna do that." But she said, No that wasn't it. She just didn't feel like wearing it. So, she kept blowing me off and I just wouldn't see. What an idiot! Even then, back then, she didn't love me and she had to keep rubbing my face in it. Everyone fucking knew I gave her that ring and she wouldn't wear it.

Rick came back to the table but he had the girl with him. I didn't think it then but now I wonder how'd he do it? How'd

75

he fucking do it? They flirted for a while without really talking or maybe he was charming her with his bad French. I even thought she was gonna start nuzzling him but she looked at her watch, then wrote something on a napkin and walked away. "Bye-bye," she said. Rick just hunched over and sucked up his Orangina through a straw without lifting the bottle off the table.

"Quit slurping," I said.

"Quit looking at me that way," he said.

"What way?"

"You're just jealous," he said and he picked up the piece of paper she'd written on and put it in his pocket. "Besides, you're the one with the chick in your lap."

Ella had her face in my neck. She was sweating all over me. "Get off," I said. When she didn't move, I pushed her. She fell on to the sidewalk. "Hey, shithead, why'd you do that?" she said. "Oh quit it. You're not hurt," I said. Rick just started laughing and he laughed and laughed and laughed until he doubled over. He took a sip and then he started laughing again so I thought he was gonna choke. I don't know what he was laughing at so hard but it made me mad. His hot red face and the big sweat stains on that preppy shirt he used to wear no matter how many times we told him it looked stupid.

When I stand up the plate smashes to the floor. I look at the cupboard and I think, I could break all these fucking dishes. There's no one here to stop me. They're stacked in there, big ones and little ones, bowls and cups. I open the window even though it's freezing out—the wind charges right through me. Then I chuck the dishes down into the courtyard, right down into the puddles and the empty planters. One after the next. They make a great crash. The African girl who lives across the way ducks into the stairway but when she sticks her head out to watch me, I chuck the last one right at her. She pulls in just in time and it hits the wall.

It works for a while. I feel lighter for a while but not for long. Soon I'm thinking about how I saw this same girl one of the first days we were here, standing in that doorway and singing. She had a turban on and a tunic and a skirt all in the same material. Yellow birds on a blue background. The birds were so bright they hurt. "Hey, can you sing louder?" I asked cuz I wanted to learn the song. It was soft, with lots of ups and downs like some weird tropical bird. I pretended to sing and opened my hands out in a big movement from my mouth but she just backed away and shut up. "Come on," I said. "Just sing it again." I started signing to show her what I meant. She turned around. When I grabbed her sleeve, she pulled away inside the building. "Oh jeez, just sing," I said. "I'm not gonna hurt you. It's nothing like that." She didn't say a word. "Come on. Why aren't you singing?" I slapped the wall with my hand but she shut the door already. She almost shut the door anyway. I could see one eye still looking out through a crack. "Catch you later," I said. I swear she smiled.

Ella was behind me. "Quit pestering the neighbors," she said. "Just leave them alone." That was her—always thought she was right, always in the fucking way. I could have had that girl too. I could have learned all her songs and a few other things—but not with Ella around.

I go out because I can't stay here, because she's here even though she's not. I don't want to think about her. She's not important. I don't need her. I never did. She wasn't right. She was wrong about everything.

"See?" I say to Ella out loud when I step into the street. 77 "What did I tell you?" Even before this break, we could go to the movies sometimes and Dave was buying wine that cost more than a dollar a bottle. "Bad idea, man," I told him and I took the bottle away. "Fuck you," he said. "Give that back to me," but he fell over the couch when he tried to grab it. Everybody laughed. Later, Ella said, "This isn't going to be funny for long. You know that, don't you? Pretty soon he's not going to be able to play and you're going to have to send him home and find somebody else." I said, "Come on, Ella. We've been together forever. We don't do that shit. We stick together. You don't know what you're talking about. He doesn't drink that much."

And I was right. He's fine. We're fine. She screwed things up.

Ahead of me on the street, one of the old neighborhood biddies is walking her dog, talking to it like it's her kid or something. All cootchie-coo in a high voice. These are the same old ladies who squeeze up behind you in the post office and read the addresses on all your letters. They take their animals into restaurants here too. I saw a dog once sitting in a chair and its old lady kept putting little tidbits on its plate.

What did she think? It was gonna take up its fork and knife? It was gonna start having a conversation with her? I could kick this one here, sniffing at every lamp post, but I don't. I just shove it with my leg as I go by. At the corner of Boulevard Voltaire, it starts raining and I start to jog. That song I'm not really working on starts going through my head again. Not "Best girl." None of that love shit. Worst girl, worst girl, shit girl. I go past the Chinese place we'd go to once a week with its big yellow sign and I throw my lighter at it. I head toward the club cuz maybe someone's hanging out there or in the record store around the corner. Jean-Marc from Les Matraques d'Amour lives around there I think. I can tell him about the record deal and how we did it all without Ella even though she never thought we could do anything without her. She set things up so we always needed her. Once Ella wasn't there when we played, and the manager screwed us over cuz he knew we didn't know French. We said, "But man, this place was packed. Guys were thrashing up on the stage and behind the bar cuz there wasn't any room, and you're telling us this is all we get?" The guy said something in French we didn't understand. He talked English til it came to money. We huddled and tried to figure out something to say, but we couldn't think of anything that'd make the manager pay us what he owed. We slammed our stuff out to the van. He just stood there and watched. At home I said to Ella, "Where the hell were you? We must of gotten screwed out of a couple thousand francs easy."

"Can't you guys do anything without me?" she said. "You knew I wasn't going to be there tonight. I even told you exactly what to say. What did you do? Forget?"

"I'm sick of this back-talk," I said. "Why weren't you there?"

"Shove it," Ella said. "I'm going to bed."

I followed her to the bedroom. "Ella," I said, "Ella, this is going good. Don't fuck this up," but she always did. And I'm tired tired tired of it. Worst girl, bad girl, dirt girl.

We were walking down a street in the sixteenth. It was late. Night. Ella was walking down one side of the street and I was walking down the other. In the middle, the streetlight reflected in the wet but we were both walking in the dark near the buildings. We were going back to the Metro from a party some French band invited us to. It was in a big bare apartment where you could see the Eiffel Tower from the bathtub. I was trying to be nice even though she was being a bitch. I said, "Hey, maybe if we stay here long enough, we can get a place like that. What d'you think?" Ella heard me. I know she did, but she wouldn't talk. All night she was ignoring me, off giggling with some chick or flirting with some other guy. If I said anything, she told me to mind my own business but if she saw me talking to some girl, she came over. "Introduce me to your new friend," she said. At eleven-thirty she said we had to catch the last Metro cuz it would cost a fortune to take a cab and she didn't want to walk clear from one side of Paris to the other. She said she didn't want to take the noctambus cuz that meant walking all the way to Etoile, then changing at Chatelet for the bus that goes to Les Lilas and we wouldn't be home til dawn. I said, "Ella, we could just stay here tonight. Maybe these guys can get us some place to play other than the dives we've been playing."

"Let Charlie take care of it. He can take care of that just fine," she said and went over and told him what to say. She told him to have a good time cuz we were leaving. I should of blown her off but I went with her.

Outside it was dark and wet. It was October. It'd been raining and I could smell rotting leaves from the Bois. I was thinking it was so cold all the he-she whores probably weren't even out in the park and they're always out. I looked up. In a black wall, there was one yellow lit window with the shutter still rolled up. Two people were there together. A man and a woman. They were just these black shapes—a black dress and black suit and black hair. Then they were one black shape. He was hugging her. Maybe they're dancing, I thought. They could be, I thought. He bent over and kissed her throat. Then I was gone. I was past them. Ella was even further ahead.

Waiting for the train, I backed her up against the tile wall. I pushed her til I heard her shoulders crunch and then I kissed her. I got my hand up under her skirt. "Cut it out," she said.

"Why? Nobody's here," I said.

"Yes. Across the way."

I turned around and saw some old guy with a bunch of flowers spraying himself with room deodorizer. That's what it smelled like anyway. He was spraying his head and the pits of his suit jacket. He kept spraying and spraying. I went

79

to the edge of the platform. I yelled across the tracks even though it was so quiet in there I didn't need to and my voice echoed, "Hey, just going on a date at midnight?" I was laughing at him and he didn't even know it. He just raised that spray can in some kind of salute and smiled. Making a fool of himself for some old woman probably. I cracked up so hard I had to bend over.

"Jesus," Ella said, "grow up."

I pushed her back from the edge. Then I grabbed her and started kissing her again. I got my tongue in there between her teeth and didn't let any air out. I shoved her until she was smack up against the wall. "Do you love me?" I asked when I got my hand between her legs again. "Do you love me? Do you? Do you?"

"Yes," she said finally.

"That's what I like to hear," I said.

SACKCLOTH AND ASHES

80

When it's been a week, I call her friends again, but they all say they haven't seen her, they don't know where she is. They all sound sorry for me, but if they knew what I was thinking they wouldn't be. When I find her, I'm gonna grab her by that long hair. I'm gonna wrap it around her throat. After a while, I think maybe they do know and maybe they're lying. Maybe at least her very best friend knows where she is. Maybe Ella's even staying with her. The next morning I go sit in the café across from her place. I drink the same cup of coffee for an hour. You can do that here. At 10:30, I switch to beer. From where I'm sitting, I can see the door. At 11, the friend comes out but no Ella. She could still be inside, I think, so I keep watching.

I think Ella, Ella, like thinking her name will make her come out so I can run across the street—and then what? I wouldn't really hit her, would I? I think Ella on the Staten Island ferry once. What we were doing there I don't know but it was after some wild night. She got sicker and sicker. We were crossing New York harbor. The waves tossed and rolled. I held her and later at my place I just let her sleep. The sky was getting light on the other side of the torn shade. She had that bitter-sour smell of old puke and sweat. She smelled like she'd eaten a bunch of those pills you take so you don't get malaria or chewed on coffee beans and aspirin. She sweated all day in my bed. I let her do that. I didn't send her home. I didn't make her sleep on the couch with the dog. If she walks out that door and comes over to me and says she's sorry, I'll be like that all the time. If she does that. Forget about caring who she talks to at parties. I'll write that love song for her that she always wanted even though she wouldn't say so.

Other girls look boring to me but I never told Ella that. A few days after I met her, I said, "I decided I don't want a girlfriend. I just wanna fuck you." I was lying but maybe she couldn't tell. "Yeah right," she said. "We'll see." I used to tease her a lot. When she wouldn't wear that ring I gave her, I said, "I don't care. Who gives a shit? What do you think I spent money on you?" It's true it wasn't from Tiffany's or anything, but it wasn't just some piece of shit I picked up either.

At 12, the lunch crowd comes into the café. They smoke cigarettes and gossip about god knows what shit but no one sits outside cuz it's gray and cold, not exactly raining. I have a ham sandwich so the waiter doesn't ask me to leave. Some days Ella would come back home at lunch time. She'd take me by the hand and pull me away while we were trying to pound out some song. She'd pull me away from the guitar and take me to the café on the corner and order salade nicoise and feed me the olives with her fingers. She'd pick them up with those red nails.

One day she came in and I was playing, working something out. The other guys were out somewhere. She just stood there watching. Started to take off her coat. "Want to go to lunch," she asked , "or stay in?" When I didn't answer, she said, "Pretty intimate with that thing, aren't you?" and pointed to the guitar. I saw how I was hunched over, looking down at my fingers on its neck. Maybe I did play too much. Maybe I worked too much, only thought about her liking my music and taking care of some of the business and sex when we got around to it. It's true when I come home, I pick up the guitar first thing. I sit down with it in my lap. That didn't leave much room for her. Even now, I get home and first thing, I pick it up.

All this time she wasn't happy, I think. All this time. The afternoon gets darker and darker. At four, the friend comes back. She glances over here but I don't think she sees me.

81

Still no Ella though. Now there're only a couple old guys in here, smoking away and drinking something cloudy. I'm sticking to beer. I didn't even know what I was doing but I wasn't making her happy. Maybe I was making her <u>unhappy</u> even. Maybe she didn't want to come here at all. Or maybe she wanted to come here but without me. I think back to when we told Izzy we were coming to Paris. Ella was in the room then. How did she look? What did she say? Izzy thought it was a stupid idea. "You guys are crazy," he said. "Listen to the shit they're playing there. You think you sound like Les Negresses Vertes or Les Rita Mitsouko? You don't sound like that. And that's the closest they have there." Maybe she said something too. Maybe she joined in and tried to tell us London would be better or Berlin or it would be better to stay in New York and we could see each other over the holidays.

If she comes out that door right now, I'll run across the street and say I'm sorry. I'll say how I won't tell her what I want her to do anymore. I'll just let her do whatever. Whatever I did that was wrong I'll stop. Maybe she left because I was screwing up with the band. She said it was gonna be Dave with his drinking but it turned out to be me. I'd yell at them all the time and then it turned out to be me. I was fucking up even back in the fall. One night I started to feel it a little, how tiny the club was and how there was no way out with all those people churning, even back in to the dark parts where I couldn't really see. Then at the bar, something caught fire. From stage I saw this flame shoot straight up, this big spurt of orange and red. I started thinking how the only door was on the other side of that whole crowd of people. I started thinking what's the word for fire in French? What's the word for help? It all kept running through my head until Charlie kicked me. He turned around, away from the crowd and mouthed to me, "What the hell's going on? You were supposed to start singing five fucking bars ago." So I calmed down. We started the song over. I told myself, There isn't gonna be any fire. Quit being stupid. And it turned out fine. We played the best ever, no kidding, and I forgot about feeling that way, but it turns out I was fucking things up even back then.

At seven, I get up and walk up and down the street for a while. I breathe in the cold damp air and blow it out again in big beery clouds. I stop in front of the Prix Unique and look at the bars of soap and the toothbrushes in the bright light but

82

I'm also looking at the reflection of the doorway across the street. No one goes in or out and after a sec I keep walking and this time, I park myself in a different café. Maybe Ella left before I got here today, I think, and soon she'll be coming back, even if it's just for a little while to change her clothes before going out again. If I even just see her for a minute, if I even just get to see her back, I'll be happy. I'll leave her alone, if that's what she wants. I'll leave Paris and I won't try to get in touch with her cuz I know I'm not worth her time. If this record breaks big, I'll give the money away. Or no, I'll save it for her, and she can decide where to give it away. When the café closes I go across the street. I ring the friend's bell and she lets me in. She stands in the middle of her place in her bathrobe, her hair every which way. It's just one little room. I can practically touch both walls when I stand in the middle of it. "You see Ella's not here," she says. "I've seen you out there all day, but Ella's not here. There's nothing of hers here. Check for yourself."

The next night is New Year's Eve. At midnight I sit in the dark and watch them light up the Eiffel Tower on TV. The date lights up in white lights, a hundred years since it was built or something like that. I remember Ella finding out about it and saying, "Oh let's go to that." "Tacky," I said. "Let's do something else." I should have said, "OK." Maybe if I'd said, "OK," she'd be here. Maybe....

83

Paris Spleen

Our place is on Rue de la Folie. "Craziness," Ella said. One Sunday she came in with a bag of croissants and dropped it on my chest to wake me up. She said, "You know, the sun's out. I don't think you've been outside during the day in weeks. I think we should go for a walk." She was right. All we'd been doing was going out at night to play or hear other people play. I fell asleep when we got home. When I woke up it was almost dark again already. I wouldn't even have known if it was weird for the sun to be out in November here. We walked to the canal and watched a lock fill up with water, then down to the cemetery. People were carrying big bunches of purple flowers to put on the graves. Ella wanted to find the people she read about. She said, "Delacroix, Proust, Apollinaire,

Modigliani, Oscar Wilde—they're all here somewhere. David, too, but I think it's only his heart. Sometime I want to get into that room where Oscar Wilde died. It's in a hotel on the left bank. I hear it's really cool, all red velvet." Even with a map, we couldn't find any of them. We kept walking up and down these paths. They all looked the same. It's another city in there with streets and the tombs lined up on both sides like houses. "Look," I said, "Abelard and Heloise. They're here. Didn't he get his dick cut off cuz he loved her?"

Ella said, "What're you trying to tell me? You love me that much? I wouldn't believe you. Besides, it's a pretty romantic view of what happened."

"Would you even miss it?"

"Shut up," she said. "What d'you think? I don't like it anymore?"

I said, "I don't fucking know. You fucking tell me. You're never in the bed the same time as me."

"You're the one who's out all night," she said. "Even the nights you don't play."

"OK," I said. "Let's go home right now."

But it didn't happen. We were walking out the gate when a girl grabbed my arm. She grabbed Ella's arm too. I couldn't tell how old she was. She could of been twelve or twenty or thirty-five. She said, "Have you seen Jim yet? You must see Jim before you go." She had some kind of weird accent, not French.

"Jim who?" I said. She looked at me like I was stupid.

"You must know Jim," the girl said. "Jim Morrison. The Doors."

"Wow. Jim Morrison's here. Did you know that Ella?"

"I forgot," she said. "Come on, let's go. I thought you wanted to go home."

"I wanna see this," I said and Ella followed me, dragging her feet. The girl took our hands. We kept making turns like being in a maze. It was getting dark, and Ella said, "Don't they lock the gates at sundown?"

"Oh sure. But you can climb over very easy," the girl said. "I have done it many times. Or you can find a tomb to sleep in. Some are like little houses, you know, and you just bring in a big pile of leaves. It's very nice."

I tried to remember some of Jim Morrison's songs but for some reason I couldn't. I remembered he died in the bathtub. I couldn't stop seeing it. Some naked guy in his bathtub and then his wife or somebody comes in and they find out he's dead.

When we got to his grave I just saw a plain stone with his name and dates and stuff people had written on it with magic marker. There were a few bunches of half-dead flowers. That's it, I thought, that's all that's left. Finally the girl said, "It was better when his head was still here." She sounded very sad.

"Someone dug up his head?" Ella asked.

"No. Oh no," the girl said. "It was a sculpture of his head. It was such a beautiful sculpture." She turned around to look at us. It looked like she was gonna cry. "Every year we meet here on the day that he died. You should come too," she said. "He means so much to us. Don't you agree?"

"Come on," Ella said, "we need you to show us the way out of here." She touched her real gentle on the shoulder, and the girl wiped her eyes. She just took off and we followed her. I noticed everything'd turned a silvery color like we'd been dipped in some weird solution that makes things glow. Everything had it. The tombs that looked like little houses. The statues of women crying and holding their hands to their heads. The trees that didn't have any leaves any more. The path. I pointed it out to Ella when we were back at the gate. "It's the moon," she said, and we both looked up at it. The girl was just standing there, waiting for something. "Hey, you OK?" I asked. "Yes," she said. "I just get so sad when I think about Jim being dead. You will come to the big party, no?" Ella said, "We'll try," and she smiled very hard, very for real. I won't see it again. I look through the tapes to find some Doors but I don't have any. Some song's right there, at the edge of my head, but I can't grab it fast enough. Dead girl, I think.

Nightmares, I've been having nightmares since she left, the kind where you wake up at four in the morning, all covered with sweat. You just know you won't sleep your heart's beating so fast, but you can't remember what the damn dream was about. Then I think, It's always gonna be this black, that's it, nothing else at all, everyone else in the world is always gonna be asleep. Other nights, I just sleep and sleep. I lie down and I'm asleep, and when I wake up I'm in the same position. Then, waking up is like trying to climb out of a hole, but the dirt keeps falling on top of me. Then when I open my eyes, the room's gray, and there's nothing to do, the whole day with nothing to do.

I go down to the Latin Quarter cuz at least there'll be people there. Behind me, there are tourists looking at postcards. I hear one of them say, "Hey didn't we see this in Rome?" and I think how stupid they are, spitting bits of information they swallowed from some guide book. But then I think at least they're here with someone, at least they're talking to someone, at least they have someone to talk to. And I just go sit in a doorway and wait to stop shaking.

On the Metro on the way home, I get a twitch in my neck. I know everyone's staring at me. They probably expect me to get up and pull out a paper cup and start telling them some horrible made-up story about how my wife died and I have six children to support, I'm suffering from some skin disease there's no cure for, I'm out of work and out of money. Back on my street, I can't stand the thought of stopping for bread even, cuz I'll have to make cheery conversation with the lady there. She'll say, "Bonsoir, Monsieur. Ca va?" and I'll absolutely have to answer, "Bonsoir, Madame. Ca va. Et vous?" And I can't stand the thought of it because nothing's ca va. Everything's for shit.

I can't eat anyways. My stomach tumbles. I can't stand the sight of food—all the tarts cut apart in the bakery windows, rabbits lying on colored leaves and shotgun casings like you're supposed to think you're finding them in the woods, those scrawny blue chickens with their heads still on, tripe and pancreas and brains and blood sausage and livers from the geese that have been force-fed. I saw somewhere they stuff the goose's mouth full with corn and hold its bill closed til it swallows, then press the food down it's neck. They do that over and over and over.

Or some days I eat too much. I eat six croissants in the morning, pain au chocolat in the afternoon. In between I go out and have steak frites for lunch. For dinner I have a whole huge platter of shellfish, one of those ones you're supposed to share, but I eat it all—the raw oysters and clams and mussels, the shrimp and the langoustes. Afterwards, I eat cheese—all different types, even goat cheese rolled in cinders. I eat the cinders. I take some with my knife and spread it on a piece of bread. I eat until I can't breathe. I keep eating anyway, even though I know cheese is gross. It's milk gone bad. It's full of bacteria. When I go to bed, I lie with my head on four pillows and feel like my stomach's going to explode. I take tiny breaths with my mouth open, like a fish in the bottom of a boat.

I just lay on the bed and look out at the apartment across the courtyard. Some priests live there, I think, but they never turn a light on. They must use candles, like they're sitting by a dead person. Later, really late, I turn on the TV. I find an old movie—*Le Baiser Qui Tue*! How appropriate, I think, *The Kiss That Kills* and watch the stupid thing for two hours. When the movie ends, I think Ella comes home. She puts a hand on my shoulder. "You're still up," she says. I turn around in slow motion. She really has gotten her hair cut and it's in a tight little ponytail at the back of her neck. She's wearing some very stylish eyeglasses, cat's eye shape, just like a real Parisian girl. She's wearing heels and a suit that's the acid green color we used to make fun of together when we saw someone wearing it. "Come to bed," she said. "You must be tired." She starts slipping clothes off, pulling me up, and somehow never letting go of my hand at the same time,

She took me to a museum once and made us stop for a long time in front of this one picture. "See," she said, "there's Marat dead in his bath. He's been stabbed through the heart even though we can't see any blood. He just looks like he's fallen asleep in the water. He looks healthy so we have to supply the details about the skin disease and the knife if we know the story. David, the painter, is dead too. And Charlotte Cordeil who really killed Marat. And everyone who saw this painting a year after it was painted, even everyone who saw this painting when it was one hundred years old. Can you believe it's still here?"

I walk around in the cemetery. I think: when the statues cry, the tears slide right down their stony cheeks. They lift the backs of their hands up to their foreheads and they have to stay like that forever.

In that square of yellow light, was that couple really dancing? He was bent over her. Maybe he was knifing her. Maybe his teeth were sunk into her neck.

There are no cheekbones I know here. At noon the sky is so bright. I hide in the house with the metal shutters pulled down tight but the light still sticks through the cracks like pins. When I go out, people seem glad to see me. Who are they?

87

I run through words I've learned: mausoleum, abattoir, noctambus, kristalnacht, Nosferatu, catacomb, sepulcher, wolfman. They run through my head and I don't know where they came from. I try to follow the paths of their sounds back to where I learned them. I can't. I have no memory. No memory except for Ella, and even she's something like spider webs. She looks solid but when I put my hand to her, there's just something sticky. When I look at my hand, I don't see anything there. In the morning, it's still dark when I go out to the café. At the counter, men are drinking their first drinks of the day. I sit at a table and order coffee and anise and start to smoke. In the big window I see my reflection. It's just a reflection of a man with a cigarette. On the table in front of him, there's an ashtray and a coffee cup.

Charlie calls. He says, "Don't talk. Don't argue with me. We're wiring you the money to come home. No, wait. Izzy says we're wiring you the <u>ticket</u> and then the money to have all our stuff shipped back. Just do it," he says. "Go pick it up at American Express near the Opera this afternoon."

It's night and Ella's here with me in bed. She is she is she is. Her hair tangled in my hands and the smoothness of her rump like a good loaf of American bread and the scratch of her fingernails on my arms and the dark shadow of her horse tattoo. We're fucking and my sweat's sliding around on that flat bone that goes down the middle of her chest. I hear her whispering, "Republique, Alma Marceau, Arts & Metier, Pasteur, Reamur-Sebastopol, Mouton Duvernet, Sentier, La Muette, Bourse,"

"What're you saying?" I ask. "Some kind of mantra?"

She sighs. "It's the Metro stops all through Paris," she says. "Come on," she says and moves her hips and starts her list again.

I like the way the French sounds, the way it swallows up all the hard sounds. "Maybe I'll use them in a song," I say. "You teach me how to pronounce them right." I start repeating what she's saying in time to how we're fucking. We're both whispering. Belleville, dead girl, Michel Ange, sad girl, Invalides, best girl. It's this double beat, double words, like two singers at once singing a map of Paris. I don't think how they're all stops on the way to get away from here. When she comes, she whimpers. She turns her face to my chest even though no one can hear if she screams. When I come, this dot of bright white light bursts into a star.

A thousand young women press up against the stage. When the singer appears, striking his guitar, pushing his dark hair out of his face, they scream, "I love you!" but their voices are lost in vibration, in music; they can't even hear themselves. They throw bras up on stage with their names and phone numbers embroidered on the cups with pink silk; they throw roses from which they have removed the thorns with a razor blade.

It's mint and red clover time in the fields here and the sweet smell comes in through all the open windows. June and the rain breaks for two days at a time, leaving a pretty blue sky. Today Joe is checking the sprinklers with his Dad, moving the ones that need to be moved, and listening to a ball game on his Walkman. I look out the window and see him do a little dance in the middle of the near field, waving his cap in the air. His team must have scored a run. I can almost hear him hoot. Inside, I have a chintz slipcover for the couch, a washer-dryer, and a new set of Corning that you can take right from the freezer to the oven to the table. Upstairs, my collection fills the second bedroom: scrapbooks with signed photos and every article on Hugh that's ever been written, a tie he wore in *Impromptu* (I really wanted one from *Four Weddings*, but that one cost a whole week's pay), a spoon with his face at the end of the handle, a pen with the name of his home town, a watch with his handsome face on the face—the dimple in his chin, his soft brown eyes—and all of his movies on video tape. I knew from the first time I saw him he'd be a star. I have it all, but the truth is I hardly look at any of it anymore, because outside I have Joe. He's got sandy hair, not dark, and the wrinkles are starting to show around his eyes, but I married him because he's gentle and kind and steady, because he found me outside the hospital in the rain, when suddenly I had <u>no one</u>, when I couldn't remember where I left my car and didn't know where I'd drive to when I found it.

A thousand young women sit on the edges of their beds. Their doors are closed; their eyes are closed tight against the light. "Oh please! Oh please!" they say under their breath and think of the same man. In the morning, they come downstairs looking as if they haven't slept—wan, distracted, disheveled. Their nightdresses are sweaty, the soles of their dancing shoes worn thin.

End of July and the fields are planted with rye grass, seed for football stadiums. Behind the fields, the hills have browned out. Behind <u>them</u>, I can see the Coastal Range, patches of fir trees and bare patches where they've cut all the trees. I look at them while I do the dishes, before I get ready to take Joe's Mom up to Portland. She's been sick, and this is the fifth time this summer I've taken her up there for a different test, a hour and a half in the car each way, her with her eyes closed, trying not to be sick. Noise makes it worse so we can't listen to the radio for distraction. It happened suddenly. She was watering her roses when I saw her double over, and I've been worried ever since—itchy and sometimes I can't sleep. They don't know what's wrong yet, and I try not to think what it all might mean. I can't stop myself though. They won't be able to fix it either: they'll give her months' worth of medicine that'll only make her sicker, and then it'll all be over anyway. Joe doesn't know this. He didn't know me yet back when my Mom and Dad were sick, both in that same hospital, both at the same time.

91

While she's in with the doctor, I read *People* and *Entertainment Weekly*. I've gotten to read every little bit this summer about Hugh's scandal, his shame. Divine Brown, I think, what did he ever see in her? But he was so sweet when he admitted he'd done something crazy, when he admitted he'd hurt the people he loved, you couldn't be mad at him for long—even his girlfriend wasn't.

When we get home, Joe and his dad are watching the Mariners' game on TV and eating chips. They've got the Weber fired up out back to put the burgers on soon's we walk in the door. "They'll figure this out, Mom," Joe says, "then they'll fix you right up." His dad doesn't say anything but he takes Mom's hand and kisses it. I mix up some iced tea and put out the container of macaroni salad we picked up at the Safeway. We eat and then the men go back to the game. When Joe's Mom goes to bed, I go read to her for a bit. She nods when I tell her about the casserole I'm planning on cooking the next night, tells me to add an ear of corn for crunch and sweetness, the kernels cut right off the cob or in winter canned is alright. When she falls asleep, Joe won't leave the game so I walk home along the road alone. It's so dark I can't see anything. I have to go by instinct, and the air is like a big warm breath.

When Joe comes in, he goes to brush his teeth and I follow him into the bathroom. "I don't think your Mom's doing that well," I say.

"She's OK," he says. "Looks like she gained back some of that weight."

"Aren't you worried?" I say.

"Course I'm worried, Norma. Don't you think I know it's serious?" He finishes brushing his teeth. Then he tells a joke the guy who fixes tractors told his dad, but at least he doesn't laugh at the end.

When he lies down, I sit next to him and try to smooth his hair with my hand. It's gotten all sweaty and twirled up from his cap. "Stop that," he says. "Stop fussing with my hair." He takes my hand and the other and pulls me toward him. "Aren't you coming to bed?"

"I'm not tired yet," I say and pull my hand away.

"Suit yourself," he says.

I go upstairs, open a scrapbook and look at Hugh's mug shot. His shoulders are all hunched up around his ears, and he looks so worn out, so pale and sort of angry, I can't stand to look at it for long. I turn to my favorite photo of him instead. He's wearing a work shirt and he's got his hand in his hair, looking right at the camera, sort of sad this time but in a thoughtful way. It's not like the other photos of him posing on some movie set with a koala bear or walking to some premiere with Elizabeth on his arm and palm trees in the background. Oh, I like those pictures too, the glamorous ones where he's all happy, but this is the real him, and he looks lost, like he's just about to cry. It always makes me sad too, to look at it, but I know if I was there, he'd tell me what was wrong, and he'd let me comfort him.

The thousand young women need to find out what type of car he drives, what his favorite food is, what brand of underwear he wears.

In a magazine, they read which city he lives in and call everyone in the phone book with the same last name, even though the calls are over-seas. They read that he didn't speak until he was four—his sister spoke for him—and they feel tender toward his shyness. They learn his band was named after his dog and they wonder who walks the dog while he's on tour. "I could do that," they think. "I could take care of his dog." They send fan letters with photos of themselves, naked. At his concerts, they buy T-shirts with his face printed on the front. When they put these shirts on, his eyes fall exactly over their nipples.

I don't know where Norma was all night. Oh, I know she was laying next to me, sleeping all curled up in a ball, but where was she? In the morning, she gets up and trips on the stairs. She makes breakfast all confused. She doesn't brush her hair or she brushes it for a whole damn hour in the bathroom. I married her because of all the girls I knew, she was the ace. This one gal, Emily, could clean the house, the whole thing, in 40 minutes flat, but she was already 0 for 4 as far as marriages were concerned. Norma, she was the one who knew how to put everything exactly where you want it, and how to find it again. Now when I ask her something, she looks round the room like she doesn't know where she is for a second. When I tell her a funny story, she doesn't even smile, tells me it's not appropriate when my Mom's so sick but I don't think that's it. That's not it at all. Besides, Mom will be OK, she has to be.

The thousand young women wish on fallen eyelashes, on birthday candles, on the first evening star; they all wish for the same thing— to meet him.

When I get to the house this morning, Joe's Mom is coughing and coughing. The sky is black with smoke from the fields being burned and behind the smoke are gray clouds. I said something at breakfast, but Joe just said, "It's September. We got to do it. You harvest, then you need to burn. The air'll be clear by the time you get home." He took his cap off, the filthy team cap I've been trying to get him to let me wash all summer, and wiped his hair back from his forehead.

While his Mom is in with the doctor, I wander up and down the hospital corridors, stop to look out over the river and all the bridges. I catch my reflection in the elevator door. Fat, I think. That's what marriage has done to me. If only my

93

mother had named me Marilyn instead of Norma. If only I'd been <u>that</u> pretty. Then I kick myself. I shouldn't be thinking such things when Joe's Mom is hearing God knows what about her fate in a room down the hall, but I keep thinking it anyway.

Outside when we leave, there's a commotion—trucks and police barricades and trailers and lights. "What's happening?" Mom asks.

"I think they're shooting a movie," I say. Suddenly my heart begins to speed. "That movie!" I remember. "He's here. I think he's here." I pull over to the curb.

"Who's here, dear?" she asks, but I just get out and tell her I'll be right back. They won't let me get near anything but I stand by a barricade and watch men and women lay cables along the ground. They're tossing rolls of black tape to each other and laughing even though it's raining.

The thousand young women take off on a summer odyssey. Sometimes, they lose track of him. They don't have the money for airplanes; they must hitchhike from town to town. When they don't have tickets for the show, they stand outside the auditorium, hoping someone will take pity on them or sell them a ticket cheap, up near the ceiling but still inside. Some of them trade sex for tickets, but the others are saving themselves for him. When he invites the audience to join him, they rush from their seats, past the security guards forming a human fence, and onto stage where he's mysteriously disappeared.

I take Mom home, but the next morning I get back in the car, with a suitcase and a sleeping bag (the one Joe uses in the fall when he and his Dad go deer hunting), and head back to Portland. At the set, they realize pretty quick that I'm not a troublemaker even though I keep asking where he is, when I can see him. "Who're you? You union?" some guy asks when I say I'll take out the trash. "I just want to get in," I say. "I just want to help." He shrugs but he lets me past the barricade. I wander around touching things he's touched and by the time I get up my nerve to find him, it's dark and the whole place is empty. Tomorrow, I think. But the next day there's a different guard who won't hear of me coming in—and the next day and the next.

Then Joe appears. He's brought his Mom up here for her appointment. "Come home right now," he says. He lowers his voice and it gets sterner. "Right now!" Part of me is waiting for him to grab me but most of me knows that he won't, so I say, "I don't think so. I think I'll stay here just as long as I please." As he backs away, I'm trembling but that night I see him, I see Hugh, walking to his trailer in the dark. Three women hover around him, holding an umbrella and a coffee cup and a notebook, all talking at once, but I run, I'm inside and when I get close to him they fade away, and just he and I are standing in the light. He stares at me with the softest eyes. "I... I just... You're great," I stammer but then I find my way. "I hope you're having a good time here. I know Portland really well—where all the good restaurants are—if you ever need a guide." I'm lying—the only place I've ever eaten is the hospital cafeteria—but it doesn't matter. I do know them, I've been to all of them. He looks at me and I know where I'd take him, what we'd do.

"Thanks," he says and squeezes my arm. This moment could go on forever but the women reappear, chattering, and men too, who swarm around and pull him away.

I stay two more weeks, watching, waiting, eating in the coffee shop at the corner, barely sleeping, following his limo to the hotel. When he gets out, he waves, and I'm sure one night he'll come over to me. "Come with me," he'll say and we go. "Do it," he says and pushes my face down to his lap, and I do. And I do other things I don't know if I'll ever do again. Ever dare do.

When the thousand young women think of him, they're making love to a swan, a shower of gold. He's better than the boyfriends they go to the movies with, better than the men who take them away for the weekend to expensive resorts, better than the lovers whose cologne smells like they imagine tropical islands must smell.

The M's are going to make the Series, and no way am I going to sit here, watching it all on TV, when she's up in Portland, following some guy who wouldn't even give her the time of day. Norma's balking, but maybe I will just run off. I put up with all those magazines piled on the toilet tank and that whole damn room full of junk upstairs when she won't let me hang even one team photo. She must think I'm a fool. One night, I saw this guy on TV. His wife was going on and on about how much she loved Elvis, how she would do anything for Elvis,

95

how she didn't believe Elvis was really dead, tears just rolling down her cheeks, and she had all the same type of knickknacks Norma does, and the whole time, her old man is standing right next to her. I thought he was one dumb fellow, sticking with this gal who's in love with some dead guy—so what if he was the king of rock'n'roll—but it turns out I'm not that different, married to someone in love with a damn movie star who got caught with his pants down, with some hooker even. It made me laugh: that guy had to pay for it!

Well, that's all over now, enough of that. As soon as the fields are burned, I'm taking off myself. They finally got themselves a great team and who knows when I'll get to see something like this again. No matter what I'm doing all day, what's happening with Mom, after dinner I can turn on the game and watch something awesome—Johnson pitching strikes or Griffey leap for a ball, almost into the stands, it seems. I can feel my legs running the bases when they get a hit. And the next day Dad and I go over it all. We complain about the bad calls and the errors. And I remember playing in high school, well nothing like that I admit, but the rush when we won.... Norma teases, especially when Dad and I spend the whole of lunch talking about one iffy double-play, but I tell myself, why should she understand?

The thousand young women write home: "I'm close. I'm this close. Don't follow me." They buy postcards in Duluth, mail them from Minneapolis on their way to catch the next train so that they can't be found.

That's it. It's over, I think as I watch them strike the set. "I need to say goodbye," I tell a girl with a clipboard. "Can I just say goodbye?"

"Oh, thanks for your concern, but Mr. Grant left yesterday," she says as she gets into a car.

I watch each and every truck drive away, and all the garbage get swept up, until everything's gone and it just looks like any city street. Then I start to drive home, stink from the paper mills filling the car even with the windows closed. I think how my mother got to see Marilyn and Joe's wedding. She stood right outside that courthouse door and saw Marilyn Monroe come out in her little blue suit with the white ermine collar, and Joltin' Joe beside her, looking happy as could be. My mother got married in a "Marilyn" dress, a white halter and an accordion pleat skirt—just like the one her favorite star wore in *The Seven Year Itch*, even though my grandmother wanted her to wear something lacy with a drop waist. My grandmother went to Valentino's funeral. She said women threw their shoes onto the coffin, touched his dead face, and tried to tear buttons from his suit. She said she saw Pola Negri swoon. The crowd filled Broadway so traffic couldn't move for miles. How loud the crying and screaming! She said she sent one of her slips to Valentino and asked him to kiss it and he did! "Oh Granny," I said, "you didn't!" but she insisted. I can't boast of anything like that. I did send Hugh a letter once. I got a photo back but the autograph had been stamped on. It looked real but when I touched it with a damp towel, it didn't smear.

Then a song comes on the radio that's so pretty I almost feel like dancing. No, I think, I won't go home. I won't. I don't have to. I have money. I have clothes with me. I have the car. This highway goes straight down to LA and I'll go there too. I'll find him. But when I hit the exit for Sweet Home, I get off as usual and follow route 20, take the turn for Sodaville, and head home. Why do I do it? For a change of clothes? But I suspect I won't leave again. He didn't once ask my name, never looked me in the face again though maybe all that was just shyness.

The house is dark even though it's near nightfall, and Joe's truck's not in the yard. All the lights are on in his parents' place, but his truck's not in their drive either. I go in and find a note on top of the TV: *Mariners made the play-offs. See you after the Series. In case you even come back and find this.*

He's gone, I think. Then I don't know what to think. I just sit down holding the note and look around. I almost forgot about the clutter. You're gone three weeks and you expect things to be different, but it's not, except now there's dust over everything too. The corners are still stacked with old almanacs, the good dishes on the pantry shelves filled with bills and receipts saved for taxes, worn-out T-shirts piled under the sink to use as rags, a dish filled with the ends of soap bars, a basket of shirts by the couch waiting to have their buttons sewed back on, an ashtray stacked with Publisher's Clearing House numbers in case we win. I pick up one thing after another and put it down again, finally settle on sorting through the tulip bulbs it's almost time to plant. I don't know what else to do with Joe not here.

97

When his Mom calls, she says, "I saw the lights on. I thought Joe was back." In the background, I can hear the TV. "Sam says I'm foolish. The game's on now and Joe will have got a ticket somehow."

We chit-chat like I was never gone, like I never spent three weeks sitting in the car near the Rose Garden, Hugh's trailer always in view, and then she says, "I hate to trouble you Norma, but could you take me back up to Portland tomorrow?"

"I'll take you. Don't worry," I say. "Nine o'clock as usual?"

When the thousand young women read his name in the newspaper, they feel they've been struck in the chest with a pole, the breath knocked out of them. The newsprint swims from the page and takes his shape—his face, his perfect teeth, his shoulders, oh his hands, his hands. They're going to faint. The next week, they read his name again: he's been seen with Courtney Love; there's a photo of them with their tongues down each other's throats.

Of the thousand young women, seven throw themselves under the wheels of fast-moving trains. One drives her car over a cliff. Maybe she was crying and couldn't see. One jumps from a third-story window, surviving a crash on to a parked car. Her bag is filled with hundreds of his photos, letters to him marked "Return to sender," and his name scribbled over every surface. Two hundred of the young women stop eating because every bite makes them ill. Three hundred of them hole up and eat nothing but chocolate chip cookies. Crumbs stick to their pillowcases, to their wet cheeks. What can they do? He was supposed to be waiting for them.

Can't believe I got to see it—the longest post-season game ever played—15 damn innings, 5 hours and twelve minutes. Then tonight, that Martinez, he slugs in two homers—a three-run shot and then a grand slam to win the game. The Kingdome was shaking. I never heard anything so loud, people stomping and screaming and clapping. All the fireworks going off—inside!—and the noise just bouncing around in there. Everybody got to be friends around where I was sitting—some parents with their kids, and two gals in full uniform, and a bunch of guys. After, some of us went for a beer, and we kept slapping each other on the back. We couldn't believe it. This one guy kept saying, "We're riding that wave. No way are we gonna lose," and we stood around outside and talked about it, long after the bar closed.

He looks out at the crowd, at the bright lights, and sees a single body, a surge of female flesh. Tears shine in the body's many eyes like oil on water. Tears of joy, he thinks; he's done that.

The next two weeks, it's like my old life, except that after supper, instead of sitting near Joe while he watches the game, I watch it myself. Really watching the crowd, I mean, looking for him. Did he paint his face blue and white? Did he buy a new cap? I can never find him. Sometimes he calls to make sure things are OK but he never leaves a number, and when his Mom's doctor decides to operate, we have no way to get in touch. The night before, we're sitting in her hospital room, the game on without sound so she can sleep. "Hey," Sam whispers, "we can do that." He's pointing to the TV. There's a Happy Birthday message on the scoreboard. Ours could say: *Joe, call home. Important.* Right during the seventh inning stretch. We call straightway to the stadium, but Joe doesn't call us. When his Mom wakes up after the operation, she asks, "Is Joe here yet? Is Joe here?" We have to say no, but at least we can tell her it was a success. "They got all of it," I can tell her. "The doctor says he got all of it." Though that doesn't mean it can't come back, I think.

At the end of the show, he drops his guitar and takes off at a run, down the aisles, up into the stands. Though he's flanked by blue-shirted security guards, each of the thousand young women manages to pull one thread from his psychedelic shirt. They put it under their tongues for safekeeping.

Then a week later Joe does come home. His truck drives up and he comes in the door, carrying a duffel bag and wearing a new sweatshirt that says American League West Champions on it.

"I'm back," he says.

We both stop, stand there, and stare at each other. I cross my arms.

"You should go see your mother." When he doesn't leave, I say, "Didn't they lose the last game a while ago?"

"Yeah, but god, what a great trip. Those games were amazing. I caught this foul ball Douglas hit, and then that same day, I saw him in the john at the airport," he says.

"You did? He's your favorite, isn't he?" In the <u>john</u>? I think. I don't say, Oh, the ugly one with the moose tattoo. "So? What did you say?"

"Nothing. I mean, it was sort of weird. We're both standing there—you know. So I wasn't gonna say anything then. And then he was done and I wasn't yet. So he leaves. What am I gonna do? Run after him? Can't stop taking a leak to shake hands. I don't really know what I would've said to him anyway." Joe puts his duffel bag down, gets himself a glass of water. "He didn't wash his hands."

I'm still just standing there, staring. "Maybe he was in a hurry," I say.

Finally he calls his Mom. Even from over by the stove, I can hear her cheer. She's so happy to have him back. He promises to visit right after supper. Then he comes over, kisses me, hugs me for a while, and it feels nice. "It's all OK now, isn't it?" he says. He sits down at the kitchen table and watches me cook. In the windows, I catch shadows, also watching—or are they walking away? When dinner's ready, we eat.

100 *Instead of meeting him, the thousand young women meet each other. "He's so gorgeous," they say when there's a break in all that sound and they pat their hearts with their hands. "Oh, when he sings that song it's like a triple orgasm." They exchange information and photos. They create fan clubs, fanzines. They construct Websites where the links radiate from a picture of him. But after all this contact with other fans, they long to be alone with him again, alone in their rooms, watching a video on MTV and waiting for the flickering split-second images of his face that they wish would just stay still. They listen to his voice feeding from the CD player through wires directly into their ears, their brains.*

A real person is there somewhere, somewhere inside the body of the star. A <u>person</u>. But insulated by so many artifacts, that person is hard to see: publicity photos, interviews, exposés, reviews of his or her work, the work itself (movies, CDs, TV shows), candid photos, magazine covers, album liner notes, appearances on talk shows, public service announcements, Websites, rumors. These allow the fan entry to the star and, simultaneously, keep the fan at arm's length. They repeat the same telling details about the star's childhood (a photo of his room filled with mementos), present life (the seven dollar haircuts), even emotional life (the long-suffering high school girlfriend who finally married someone else), until they construct a persona that's remarkably consistent. The texts reassure—reinforcing what the fan already knows, assuring one that one <u>does</u> know the person who is the star. But most of these texts also add a new detail—a current love interest, a favorite sport or hobby, a snippet about where the next movie or recording is being made—and so maintain the fan's curiosity. And this new information raises doubts about how much we do know, necessitating that we buy this magazine or tune in later for the full interview in order to rectify our knowledge or accumulate more. Despite all this, we're also, always, aware of our ultimate lack of knowledge, an odor of deprivation. Whole realms are inaccessible: the photo never lets us see the back of the star's head. We never get to smell him, despite those perfumes that claim to contain a drop of the star's sweat in each bottle. And sometimes the repetition of information seems calculated rather than revelatory—a wall built up to protect the star rather than details that reveal the person inside. Once we start to think this way, all the documents become suspect, their very consistency becomes suspect. Even the most melancholy photo, the one we're at first sure can't be posed—hand in hair, gray ocean and sky in the background—becomes suspect. That sadness is just another come-hither look. I realize that I only know one side of his face—the left—that someone has decided this is his "good" side. It's light like silk that idealizes his body, that gleams in his blue eyes, and shines off the dark hair swept off his forehead into a pompadour. (Don't our fantasies entail the destruction of that perfect hair... There's no hairdresser to recomb it when we're there, alone with him.) But these documents are all I have to go on—and I consume them, insatiably. I study the backgrounds of photos for clues, compare articles and interviews for inconsistencies, search for the flaw through which I can see the real person. And I'll find him because there's a mysterious and secret communication between star and fan, between him and me, which can't be controlled. No, don't worry. I'm not going to show up on his doorstep with a gun. I know there are rules that govern the relationship between us, a code that keeps me longing in private, but I'm also sure that some day, you'll pick me out of the crowd at a concert; that I'll run into you on the beach (the one where they shot that video—you must really go there to surf) or at the grocery store buying anything but tomatoes (I know you don't like those); that you'll call back when I finally find the right number.

The thousand young women all know the same thing: his song is his voice and his voice is his breath and his breath comes pushing through his lips, teeth, and tongue, comes streaming up out of his throat from his lungs, and his lungs work only because his heart beats blood through his body. And so to listen to his song is to follow his breath back down inside his body, to touch the spit-slick back of his throat and swim in his blood.

MEMENTO MORI

AND SO I HAVE RETIRED, although I am quite sure I would not have used that word immediately upon returning from my last adventure to this mid-sized house in the middle of nowhere—the family home, isolate, set now among empty fields like a ship in the middle of the ocean. Some days I am sorely tempted to stitch the bedsheets together, hoist them, and set sail. I did know that shortly after my arrival, I would be joined by my elder brother Arthur, who, having endured our mother's and then our father's interminable terminal illnesses (wherever I traveled, I found a letter forwarded to me, detailing the latest surgery, radiation treatment, chemotherapy, vitamin therapy, or diet—detailing its failure), had taken off on what he claimed was an adventure of his own—some hopelessly effete tour of the monuments of Europe. And I knew that a few weeks later, our sister Martha would join us for the Christmas holidays, accompanied by our niece and twin nephews, the boys five and the girl fifteen. But I did not know that I, the boy who had escaped, would be staying on here alone.

I believed I was merely resting before the next adventure, coming home to catalogue the objects I had collected during nearly thirty years of journeying and to renew acquaintance with the family I had certainly neglected. Oh, I had written them—postcards from each port of call—but mostly they'd learned the details of my exploits from the articles I wrote. (I'd seen no need to trouble them with more particulars than they could find there.) The doctor had prescribed several months' ease in a moderate climate to recover from the hardships of my expedition to Everest (a touch of frostbite, some lingering parasite, a strained knee, and a case of high-altitude pulmonary edema). I had saved the tallest of the tall mountains for last and was now allowing myself to indulge in some months of well-deserved rest. I imagined spending the holidays quietly if a bit dully with my relatives, and then, after the new year, planning my next expedition in order to alleviate the boredom I expected to encounter in this sedate landscape and settled climate. Here, winter comes but brings no great freeze, no blizzards, no encrustations of ice. Instead, the season is marked by a series of soft days when the horizon—such as it is—fades into the sky, and the trees seem drawn against the gray clouds in a slightly darker shade of gray. The dull ground is sometimes covered by a thin layer of gritty snow. Spring is as innocuous: trees bud tiny leaves and a few crocuses push up through the dirt. Summers are mild, nothing more than the same landscape clothed in relentless green, and fall is marked by the leaves turning a pale yellow, then brown, then falling to form a thick slippery layer that dulls all sound. Even in childhood, I remember remarking on the indefinite character of the climate here, as if Mother Nature knew she should be changing seasons but had barely the energy to do so.

104

And so, on a fall day almost exactly a year ago, I followed the road from town, the long drive through fields and pastures now let out to other farmers, acre after acre of stubble. At the house, the two oaks still stood, one on either side of the front door. We'd had a swing in the one on the left and I half-expected to see my siblings there, for, aside from an exterior coat of paint the odd clotted color of spoiled milk, the place looked exactly the same. Inside too, not much had changed: some stereo components now sat on an incongruous set of pressed wood shelves in the parlor, but I found all else the same, if a bit shabbier—the same rose-trellised wallpaper in the hallways, the same Morris chair and settee covered in dark green velveteen, the same Rheem-Wedgewood range in the kitchen, and the same pull-chain commode in the watercloset. Upstairs, my old room looked much the same as well. The curtains were drawn, but when I slid them open, they revealed the view I had stared at for so many hours as a youth, wondering what lay on the other side of the hill. Then the heat began to knock in the radiator and that old feeling of entrapment returned. I'd always found the house intolerably stuffy and all winter opened windows, propping them up with piles of books I didn't much want to read anyway, and my mother followed around behind me closing them. When I was thirteen, our quarreling became so constant, my father finally agreed to nail the windows shut, even the ones in the attic. "We really need some ventilation up there," he said but she'd insisted. That morning she'd found her African violet touched by frost. At night I'd kick the covers off, peel back the sheet, unbutton my flannel pajama jacket, and sleep with my arms and legs spread, reveling in the kiss of cold air, but my mother had always come into the room at midnight and covered me again. It had been a long time since I'd remembered these things, after so many years sleeping when and where and how I liked, but the close room and the failing autumn light reminded me. I remembered her gooey smell, as if she'd bathed in tapioca pudding, and I sat down on my old bed and put my head in my hands.

Over the next few days, I unpacked my collection (the crates had been stacked in the basement, next to the deep freeze which now held snow from the North and South Poles), calling in a couple of men from town to help me with the larger items. We set the Bengal tiger in the front hall, and placed the sea creatures on the dining room sideboard — the urchins, the giant squid, the poisonous jellyfish, the terrific jaw and teeth of a great white shark. The rocks, one from each continent's highest peak, I arranged on the parlor mantle, taking the newest, from Everest, out of its cotton batting myself and setting it in the very center, the place of honor. On the shelves nearby, I arranged the vials of sand, one from each of the world's deserts, and the specimen bottles of water, one from each of the world's oceans. And in the upstairs hall, ordered one after another, I placed the cases of moths (rosy maple moths, sagebrush sheep moths striped like zebras, and Io moths with gray and black eyes staring from their hind wings), of ants and crickets, and of bird wings. (Each wing has been extended so that one can see the linings and coloration usually seen only by other birds in flight. Each wing is a different shape for a different purpose: hawk and prey with short round wings for maneuverability; the owl's wing large for slow, well-supported flight; pointed wings of the swallow and tern for rapid flitting; and my favorite, the albatross, whose long narrow wing stretches across the entire top of the case, excellent for long distance gliding.) In the attic, I hung a hammock. I could seek refuge there when I tired of my family.

105

I would pry open the window and hope for a great wind to rock me.

When my brother arrived, I was surprised to recognize him: the wide-set gray eyes, the pointed nose. Had anyone asked, I would not have been able to summon an image of him, but I knew his face immediately. My God! The same person! And, as when we were young, he immediately began to pummel me. He thumped me on the back and patted my graying hair—all gestures I abhorred but suffered with dignity, I hope. Or perhaps I was too busy being astounded by my brother's resemblance to our father to respond.

After supper, we took a walk around the house, discussing this and that. I'd turn to look and, again, see my father in a dismissive hand gesture, hear him in the midwestern inflection of 'roof,' the word turned into the barking of a dog. In every room, he asked about the items displayed there, then as quickly, turned to another subject. When we sat down in the parlor, he asked me again to tell him how I had acquired the objects. "Nothing really, just some curios collected on my travels," I said. "No, really, how did you get your hands on these things," he said. When he leaned very close, (I thought, then, that his eyes took on the suspicious look of certain snakes, but now I am sure he was merely curious, excited to have someone in the house with him, someone to converse with), I decided to oblige him, but when I mentioned sailing through the frozen Circumpolar Current, he moaned about battling crowds at the Uffizi; when I described traveling by camel through the Gobi Desert, he recalled the insults of French waiters (he laughed and said he'd heard that camels, too, tend to hiss and spit); and when I told of eating beetles in the Amazon, he complained of suffering through meals of soggy cabbage and boiled beef in England. He bragged and bragged of the hardships he had faced, and when finally we climbed the stairs to bed, I was sorely tired, after adopting, for hours, the affectation of a grin. I, of course, could have out-boasted him (those had been mighty storms when Antarctica was the closest land and I alone in the boat; that camel he ridiculed had been my only companion in the desert and I'd had a single ripped map for guidance; I'd eaten beetles in Brazil because they were the only food—I'd have starved otherwise), but there seemed little point. I remembered the humiliations I had faced daily as a child when he surpassed me in every school subject

106

and even snatched my report card away so that he could show it to our father alongside his own perfect one. I had faced hazards simply because they were there. At most, the sense of danger provided a spurt of energy which helped me to achieve a goal, but otherwise the perils served no purpose at all. My brother, however, reveled in recounting every unpleasantness he'd encountered.

We spent the next weeks largely separate and silent (now I might call it a companionable silence; then I was not clear what to call it and may even have found it sinister), except for the time we spent reviewing our father's estate. It seems he'd had some business sense after all, and there shall be a tidy sum for each of us and trusts for the grandchildren, once it's all put in order. My brother had expressed the wish to live anywhere but here and so the house has been left to me. Then, finally, the big day came—a week before Christmas—and I had high hopes for my sister Martha's company. As children, she'd been the intercessor, the devisor of games on rainy afternoons, the packer of picnics on sunny ones. When she and her children arrived for their two week vacation with more suitcases and parcels than I took for a year's trip around the world however, my hopes began to sour. Then she swept me into a great strangling hug. "Oh, Gordon," she said, unable to contain tears. Behind her, I saw the niece and twin nephews I'd never met. The girl stared, an ice doll wrapped in a rabbit fur jacket, and the boys seemed maddeningly, wickedly identical. My sister introduced us. "This is your Uncle Gordon," she said, "and this is Bernice and David and Martin."

"Martian! He's a Martian, not Martin," one boy shouted— it must have been David—and the two ran off, stooping to gather some of the thin snow into balls which they then threw at each other. "Boys!" Martha said and laughed. "That's just how they are. But you haven't had any children of your own, have you Gordon?" I winced but, really, she was right. "Come then," she said, tucked her arm under mine and led me back inside.

After a dinner accompanied by the boys' raucous chatter, I found Bernice back in the dining room, staring at my collection of sea oddities. She jumped when I cleared my throat. "Such a pretty color," she said. "See, it matches my dress." And she was right. She grasped the fabric of her full skirt in one hand

107

and held it up for me to inspect more closely; it was the same gauzy blue as the jellyfish she'd been staring it in its jar of preservative (little did she know its sting could kill a man in four minutes). She leaned close to the jar and her hair, peculiarly almost as pale as her skin, reflected the watery fishy blue so that she was all blue, an apparition. Who else had hair so pale, skin so fine? Roxanna perhaps? Then she straightened and spun slowly, gazing at the walls, at the photos of all my trips, of the partners I'd traveled with and the women who'd waited for me at the ends of my journeys, and the likeness faded. "My mother said it was just an old farmhouse, but it's like a natural history museum here," she said with wonder.

"Come, my dear." I smiled and touched her lightly on the arm. "We're having coffee in the living room. You should join us. Your mother has even let your brothers stay up late."

That night, we exchanged small talk, bits of gossip, news of long lost cousins and friends. Arthur and I exchanged quips about the teachers we remembered from primary school while the boys got more and more fidgety and Bernice sank lower and lower in her seat. Finally she burst in, taking advantage of a pause in our talk. "Oh, please, Uncle Gordon, won't you tell us about your adventures?"

"Really, there's nothing to add to what you've read. I included everything of importance."

"He says you went to the moon," one of the boys said, pointing to his brother.

"No, not the <u>moon</u>, stupid. I said..."

"Now, Gordon," their mother interrupted, "there must be details you didn't include. You must tell us everything, all the things you wouldn't dare report in those magazines."

"At least tell us about Everest. We haven't read about that trip yet," Bernice said.

That was true. I'd yet to write the article. I might even think of this as a dry run. And so I told them about the climb up Everest, how in the Khumba Ice Fall, I had found a great lip of overhanging snow like the frozen breath of God. And below, a chasm of slick, emerald green ice. I'd barely been able to leap across it and secure my ice ax in the other side. From the summit, a plume of snow blew. The mountain breathed. And in only a few days, I was on top in the midst of that breath, the flags of spindrift, the sky bluer and clearer and more pristine than anywhere else on earth. My family breathed long and hard as I told them about this climb. Bernice chewed her lower lip, her mother clutched her coffee cup and exclaimed, "Oh, how dreadful!" whenever I described a difficult traverse. Telling the story, I savored the memory of action, body pushed to its utmost. I see now that on that climb, as on my climbs of all the High Seven mountains, I cherished most the meditative state I was able to enter — measuring breaths in the airless air, fighting cold and wind and the sharp squint of sunlight, crampons jammed into the ice so that I balanced above nothing, swinging step after treacherous step until even the ache in my limbs disappeared — my concentration was honed so sharp that I could leave the petty concerns of daily life behind: how I might fund the next expedition, where I might spend the next break between trips, why I had suddenly received a spate of letters from my father demanding that I return home.

"But weren't you afraid?" Bernice asked when I had finished by describing my descent and the welcoming embrace of my companions waiting below.

"Fear? Fear is merely a physiological response," I said, "Fight-or-flight — just a rush of adrenaline, an increase in heart rate and blood pressure, the muscles at alert. And besides, if one keeps one's head, there's little to fear. Deaths in the wild are almost always due to human error. Preparation is everything." I told them how my own only brush with death in the mountains had been due to altitude sickness: headache, shortness of breath, nausea, as lungs and brain swelled. It was a result of my own willfulness, my insistence on climbing too fast, and then as I continued on and on, up and up, my condition deteriorated, I explained and shook my head. "Only once I coughed up a substance that was frothy and colored pink by blood did I realize I must descend so that I might recuperate and start over." I watched my family finally sit back in their chairs. I watched them sigh and wipe their brows, but I was feeling, finally, after weeks of inactivity, full of energy, and I remember I had trouble falling asleep that night.

Our visit proceeded with all the usual holiday festivities — a trip to town to see the lights, calls upon old family friends who once again gave us their condolences on our father's passing and hungered for stories of my adventures, the Christmas eve decoration of the tree, the Christmas morning opening of presents. And at night, before I went to sleep, I'd flip a switch in the hall and let the crickets trill; I often found myself wishing I had only those noises for company rather than my family's relentless chatting, the two women nattering (buzz buzzing in the next room like flies against glass when they've woken in a winter warm spell), the boys' endless screaming matches and bouts of giggling.

Late on Christmas afternoon, with everyone else sleeping off the rich midday meal, I came upon Bernice in the front hall, eyeing the tiger (this creature whose very essence I have preserved, much more than a stuffed trophy). I watched her bend over the beast, holding her long blond hair out of the way with one hand. In our conversations, she'd seemed a typical if bright adolescent, but as she rubbed the tiger's head luxuriously, scratched behind his ears, ran her hands over the flanks—dark brown striping on reddish orange fur—I wondered if we might possess a deeper connection, share a certain curiosity and daring, a sensuousness nature. Be careful, my dear, I almost said, my heart speeding, but instead I stood half-hidden by the dining room door and wondered whether she would discover the switch hidden on his creamy underside. She did! I heard the barely audible click as the mechanism, exact and superb, was activated, and then I waited, breath held, for the stuffed tiger to come alive, all ten feet of him, all 500 pounds. His skin and fur were warming, I thought, and soon.... And soon.... Unaware, Bernice stood calmly next to him, rubbing his nose, but when he began to exude his musky, wild-cat smell, she sniffed, stepped back, a puzzled look on her face. I watched the comprehension come, the fear flit—a shadow behind her eyes. I timed my breaths to hers as we both watched the tiger open his mouth and yawn a deliciously deep and terrifying yawn that exposed all his sharp white teeth. At that, Bernice gasped. She cowered against the wall, afraid to move, but I knew it would be a few moments still before the tiger realized his hunger and stepped from his pedestal. First he would growl—and how might she react to that? Then he did growl, a low rumbling from deep in the belly. One might even mistake it for a purr, as if the tiger had died and a housecat been reborn in his body. Indeed, Bernice almost smiled as she edged her way to the door, but the tiger kept moving and her fear returned. He stretched. He yawned again. He lifted one paw and I leapt forward, reached beneath his belly, and stopped him. I shivered, not realizing I had broken into a tense sweat. "There," I said and backed up until I stood next to my niece. We watched the tiger recompose himself, the mechanism winding down just as it had been created to do.

"Did.... Did you make that?" Bernice asked.

"I found him, my dear, as I found and brought back all the things in this house." I drew her away from the beast, but she eyed it over her shoulder, then sat her down on the bottom step where we could watch him through the bars of the banister and circled her shoulders with my arm to stop her trembling.

"You captured him?" she said.

"Well, yes," I said and told her the story I believed she wanted to hear. "I found him in Burma, in the jungle. My guide led me into the mountains, day upon day of stealthy march, far from civilization, for hunting tigers is highly illegal." Bernice looked at me, startled. "At last, late on the third day, just as the dark shadows stretched their longest across the ground, just as everything took on the striped appearance of a tiger's hide, he struck his arm out across my chest and stopped me. For the longest time, I held my breath and I believe my guide did the same for I heard only the much slower, larger breath of the entire forest in the growing dark. I sensed a change, though, some subtle quieting of birds and beasts. Even the shadows, the last golden rays of sun, and the dark green leaves seemed to stop moving. Then I saw the tiger. He carried himself forward with a fluid weight-shifting gait, shoulders rolling, paw pads lifting and dropping silently, and when he stopped, he disappeared, his camouflage was so perfect. We stood absolutely still until I was just able to distinguish his stripes from the shadows. I moved slowly, raising the gun, all the while praying that the tiger would remain in his crouch, eyeing a deer that seemed unaware of his presence. I could see his flanks move with his breath, his whiskers twitching, and then in an instant, deer sprang, tiger leapt after it, and I fired. The explosion tore through the forest, shaking birds from their perches, scattering smaller beasts, and the tiger fell, hit the forest floor with a crash, flapped his tail a few times, and died." I looked at Bernice and saw she felt the same excitement I'd felt when facing the tiger, the hair rising on the backs of both our necks: she had slid away from

111

me and sat ready to leap at any moment. "It's delicious, isn't it?" I said. I seized her hand. "You understand, don't you, how I feel, how horrendous it is to be trapped in this house after living a life like that." Suddenly Bernice became a flurry of energy. She hurried to the living room, gathered her presents of scarves and hairbrushes and sweaters and the necklace I'd given her of a beetle suspended in amber, and ran up to the room she was sharing with her mother as if preparing for some great adventure. I did not see her for the rest of the evening.

After that though, there occurred what I now recognize as a reticence on my siblings' part and on Bernice's (truth be told, she seemed to avoid me, even though I'd saved her from the tiger), a tendency to look the other way when I spoke. The two boys showed no such lack of interest, however; indeed, they seemed to become more and more attached to me. One evening they came to find me in the attic where I lay alone in my hammock as I'd taken to doing while my relatives played some game I had no interest in: Scrabble or backgammon or chess or Mah-Jongg. My sister always asked—I must say that—if I wanted to join them. After a day, no days, of madcap chases, fights where they flailed at each other with the empty sleeves of their jackets, and games of cops and gangsters, punctuated by the sound of rapid spitting—their imitation of machine gun fire, the boys were strangely quiet. "Tell us a story, Uncle Gordon," one of them said (I still have no idea which one, as their mother persisted in that horrendous habit of dressing identical twins in identical clothes). I found a chair, then pulled one up onto each knee. "Let me tell you about my journey to the bottom of the sea," I said, but as soon as I began to tell them how dark it is down there, as dark as when you crawl under the covers in the middle of the darkest night of the year, as soon as I mentioned the blind fish and the albino octopus, they grew fidgety, and once I began to explain how the sandy bottom is the inverse of deserts up above, lacking light, not water, they began to interrupt:

"Did you have a wet suit? How did you breathe? Were there monsters? How did you see the fish if it's so dark?"

I answered their questions as best I could, but they would not listen. One boy (the one seated on my left knee—it must have been David) said, "Martin's scared of the dark. He makes us sleep with the light on." "Am not!" the other replied. "Are too!" The quarrel continued, and then they began to tussle, reaching across me to slap at each other. "You know," I said, prying them apart. "I used to be afraid of the dark, but you must conquer it; you must face it head on. You see, if your eyes are clouded by fear, you'll not be able to appreciate the wonders you come across." They calmed for a second, then began again, to kick each other now, harder and harder, until it was impossible to hold them. "Off, boys, off," I commanded and stood up, but they refused to leave me alone. One grabbed hold of my trouser leg and hid behind me while the other batted at him. After a few minutes of this struggle, they tore free, chased each other, and then returned, the other taking his place behind me, his brother now on the offensive. "Come boys," I said, in a fit of irritation, "if you're good and quiet, I'll devise some adventures for us to pursue."

They bombarded me with questions, but these, at least, kept them from attacking each other, and I was able to lead them downstairs and hand them over to their mother who gave me a worried look.

Over the next few days, my nephews became my untiring companions, my sturdy followers, as we visited my own favorite boyhood haunts—the frigid fishing stream clogged with dead leaves, the high water tower I'd often climbed— and even some new sights in the area—an auto junkyard full of rusty hulks, the building site for a new mall at the edge of town with steep sides to slide down, Indian ruins a farmer had discovered when digging foundations for a barn and now charged two dollars to see. I grew accustomed to the boys' pestering questions, their incessant senseless prattle, and they way they'd run at me from a great distance and then hurl themselves against my thighs. And so when, at bedtime the night before they were to leave, the boys could not be found, I was the first to respond. "I'll look for them," I said and took my coat off the hook.

But my sister said, "No, not you, you've done enough," and I put the coat back down on a chair. "You started this in the first place. You've taken them off on some 'adventure' every day this week, and now they've gone off like this. You'd probably just take them further into the woods." She started to sob on my brother's shoulder. "Arthur, you call the police," she said, but she clutched him so tightly, he couldn't get to the

113

phone, and Bernice just chewed her lip and dried the dishes. Since no one else seemed ready to hunt for the boys, I headed out, even though my plan hadn't been sanctioned. And perhaps I <u>had</u> instilled an unhealthy sense of daring in them and so was somehow responsible for their flight, although I had taken them on mere rambles really—and I had always made sure we had enough warm clothes and a thermos of hot sweet tea.

Out in the orchard, the temperature was just above freezing and a fine stinging rain fell steadily. Behind me, the house lights reflected off the low clouds with a peculiar glow, and when I turned around, I could just make out the harsh, distorted silhouettes of the trees. I could smell rotting apples, putrid and dense. No one picked them anymore so they simply fell to the ground and decayed. I reminded myself that on top of Everest I'd stood alone, well away from the hundreds of other climbers down at base camp. I'd reached the summit without oxygen, quite a feat. The sky all around was a brilliant blue dusted by dry windblown snow, snow fine as the aspirin tablets my father would grind into a powder when we were children and then press directly into a wound. And the snow glittered, pin-prick and opalescent. For a second the wind dropped to silence, and I thought the mountain buoyed me like a flag. But I must find the boys, I told myself. Where would they go? Where were they headed? I tried to remember the direction I would have taken myself as a boy, out into the wild, out into the night when I didn't want to be bothered with adults, but all the orchard rows looked suspiciously alike. I followed the rise and fall of the land, and once I reached the other side of the hill, there was no light at all—no moon and the clouds covered the stars, even the lights from the house had disappeared. There was only a blackness—neither the close black of a cave nor the thick black of an Amazon night but a blackness never-the-less and the sense that the trees were watching. I stood quietly for a moment, breathing lightly so I might catch any sound of the boys, then hurried on. I thrust aside brambles that had grown up among the trees and slogged through long dead grass. And I rushed on through a growing mist, air that got thicker, gummier, colder, propelled by the fear that I would not find my nephews. Coming down from Everest (even breathless in my descent, the first clue that something was truly wrong with my lungs), I passed the colorful tattered remains of tents, discarded oxygen cylinders, human excrement, and finally a corpse. I looked down in a crevasse and there it was, the frozen face staring up at me, yellow skin tightened to the skull, some climber not as lucky as I, lost in a whiteout perhaps, hypothermic. Thoughts muddied, I may even have stumbled in circles until I found the boys merely by chance, by the sound of their chattering teeth. The fools had set out dressed only in their matching footed pajamas and were soaked now, though huddled well beneath the boughs of a pine (at least they'd thought of that shelter) at the edge of the forest. I took one under each arm like a damp puppy and felt them shivering fiercely against my sides. Afraid they'd slip from me into shock, I ran back up the long hill to the house, ran so fast I forgot the breathlessness that had been plaguing me. Was this the adventure I'd been training for? "You're safe. You're safe now," I told them.

Back at the house, Martha opened the kitchen door when I kicked it with my boot. She took the twins, placed them down, and pushed them behind her. The light was so bright I had to shield my eyes with my hand, wished for snow goggles. "We called the police," she said. "Why couldn't you just wait for them to come? They're out there now." She glowered, then called over her shoulder to my brother.

How long had I been out there in the dark and damp? When I'd left—it seemed merely a half hour before—my family had been paralyzed, unable to take the situation in hand, and now, so soon, they'd called the police, the police had set up a command post in the dining room, dispatched their dogs and officers. I had no idea why she was so disturbed. What edict had I broken when I'd saved her sons from the night? The boys began to pull on their mother's skirt, to yammer and interrupt each other's exaggerated accounts of their adventure, fabricating wild dangers (monsters and demons that fed on the dark) and ignoring the real and much more present ones (wet, cold, loss of direction), but Martha just said, "In the morning. You can tell me in the morning," and took them off with Bernice for a hot bath and bed. Arthur passed them in the doorway, a policeman in a firmly pressed, dark blue uniform just behind him. "Ah, here he is," my brother said, "the one-man rescue party." Did he actually smirk? He turned to the sergeant, turned his back to me. "I'm very sorry we've put you to all this trouble," he said.

"Important thing's the kids are back safe. Though if we'd known you had such a crackerjack on the premises, we could have saved ourselves the bother," the policeman said as my brother escorted him outside. I heard the door close, and the house became strangely silent.

The next morning, I watched as my family walked out to the car together, a huddled, disheveled group, my brother seeming to shelter them all from my gaze, his arms spread wide. The two little boys stole backward glances and at the last moment, my sister returned to place her cool palm on my cheek. "I'll write," she said. "And you'll come visit, perhaps when the boys are older." Bernice ducked her ice blond head into the car, and then, to my surprise, my brother piled his suitcases on top of theirs in the trunk and got into the car with them. I knew he'd be leaving but not so soon. I assumed we'd have weeks together yet while he decided which city to relocate to. He hugged me briefly, patted me on the back, and gave me a look that irked me no end with its false piety, its pity.

Now sometimes, when I wake in the middle of the night, gasping (the sensation that no matter how deeply I inhale, the air cannot find its way past a sticky valve), the empty house feels like a dark ship, one of those ghost ships I saw during my crossing of the Pacific—pirates perhaps but in any case unwilling to answer my horn or my flares, riding the sea without lights. Then I took it as a challenge: I'd make my way alone. On Everest, the snow field was steep, heavily crevassed, and up above, on the higher reaches of the slope, a layer of insubstantial snow lay over hard ice, but I'd charged on. Now I remember the chasms below me, dark and very deep, and even my solid bed in this solid house seems perilous. During the day, I plan a lecture. I take phone calls from my agent and requests for advice on outfitting an expedition. At night, the rooms glow with a darkness that's the opposite of sunlight, and the corpses wake me, not just the one corpse but all the bodies left on Everest, frozen monuments propped against a serac—the last place they sat down—or interred under tons of avalanche-driven snow. The quiet presses upon me, just exactly as if my two young nephews had playfully stuffed their fingers in my ears. I rise from my bed and wander the house, dragging the green metal oxygen canisters behind me on their cart. My injured knee is stiff and I stumble from room to room, turn on lights, but the displays are silent. I must have known that one day, these souvenirs would be all I had to remind me of the places I have been, of <u>who</u> I have been (unlike those other founders of museums—Sir Walter Cope with his castle, or Ashmole with Tradescant's collection, or Calceolari, or Imperato—I have collected <u>myself</u>), but it turns out they are poor company. At each relic, I stop and recall how I acquired it, how I shot the birds, captured the moths, dug the rocks from frozen slopes, but always I have forgotten some elusive, essential part of the story: the sensation is gone. I return to my room, to the blue light of the television, and wind the tin and plastic toys the boys gave me for Christmas— the spinning circus elephant, the yellow tractor from Czechoslovakia pulling its own combine, the hopping guitars and eyeballs, and the lumbering dinosaur, just so that I can listen to them clack and rattle against the floors.

Sometimes I see Bernice's hand hover over the urchin's poisonous spines. I could have pressed it down, pressed the spines into her flesh until her pretty pink palm was pricked with a dozen pinpoints of bright blood, then sucked the blood away before the toxin, a nerve poison, had a chance to travel far, before the poison could reach her lungs and she would stop breathing—not because she <u>couldn't</u> breathe but because each breath would cause such a refined agony that she would choose not to breathe. I did none of that. She would not die that death. I see Bernice holding the urchin in the palm of her hand. We are underwater together, on the rocks where I found the specimen—phylum Echinodermata. It waves its long spines languidly; it scrapes its beak, the five hard plates of Aristotle's Lantern, across her palm searching for algae. It tickles her and she smiles at me.

Roxanna—how old would the child be now? Bernice's age perhaps? I've written, asked you to send photos, but you don't respond. At night I try to place that visit, locate it between adventures, but I can't. It slips. One moment I remember myself in your bed, Roxanna, during the hiatus between two trips across the Pacific (I recall your smoothing a cool lotion onto sunburns so severe the skin blistered), but then I place it after some other trip on which I might also have gotten so burned—the trek across the Gobi? Or one of the other deserts? Perhaps even that simple fishing trip I took after descending McKinley. I find I can remember the

117

expeditions well enough, but the spaces between them float in a liquid sea of time.

At breakfast the morning they left, I told my family about storms in the Pacific, alone at the helm of my sailing boat while the ocean fumed and roiled around me, and then I leapt up to retrieve the shark's jaw from the sideboard, to show them its fearful teeth. I dove into the darkest parts of the ocean. I hunted deadly animals in the darkest jungles with only native tools—a bow and arrows so fine I wondered how they could withstand the force of piercing skin or blowdarts coated with a poison I only half-believed would subdue an elephant. I persevered through a long trek across the ice cap to the pole with only my sled dogs for company. I'd left too late in an unusually warm spring and the ice opened before me, the dark water swallowing the lead dogs. I was just able to pull the others back. I spent three nights alone in a bivouac bag hanging from the north face of the Matterhorn while a blizzard raged. I talked and talked, told story after story until I was winded, while they all, the five members of my family, the five people closest to me in the world, passed the sugar and milk, bowed their heads over their cereal bowls and prepared to leave.

DOWN PAST MECCA THERE is a tremendous inland sea. I know because I've seen it, the Salton Sea, stretching way across the desert valley in the morning, flat and blue. I drove there all unawares, a series of accidents—*farblondjet*, Mama would have said, *like a chicken with her head cut off*—but now I'm going back. "Meshugge," my older sister Rose said when I told her. I was on my way to visit her when I saw it first. "What do you need it for?" she said. Yes... but I'm on my way now, driving from the two bedroom in Santa Monica that she wanted me to share. Something happened there, in Santa Monica, where the ocean glittered, and the palm trees waved and rustled, and the crowds of young people biked and skated and bared their bellies. Or maybe something happened in the desert— before I even got to the ocean. But today, after a week of Rose insisting I live with her—"the best place in the world," she said; after a week of mornings sitting on a bench, waiting for her friends to find us and chat; after a week of afternoons with Rose first asking for a magazine, then a book, then the television on, then off, then the radio tuned just to one particular station and a nice hot cup of tea, I fled. I got back in the rental car and drove east, through one suburb after another, past the exit for Disneyland.

When I was in New York, my niece Phyllis called—the hysterical one—and then my nephew Danny—the doctor like his father: "Come. Your sister Rose needs you. She's been so difficult since Dad died."

"Of course I'll come," I agreed. I am alone, after all, the healthy sister, the one without any obligations, and I felt sorry for them—so many years of their mother looking after them and now they had to look after her. I knew what that was like. I had been the one to take care of Mama. And both of them busy with their own lives: the children, the work, the husband away on business for six months overseas. And I had just retired after 35 years of service, given a gold-plated pen by Mr. Jenson and a chocolate bar in the shape of a typewriter. Just before Passover, I left for the desert. I left my bookcases in New York, the set of Dostoevsky I've been saving to reread, and flew to Phoenix. There, for a week I stayed with our cousin who's turned the desert into a beautiful garden just like the one she tended in New Rochelle. Beautiful roses— "They grow even better out here," she said, "as long as you water them enough." In the mornings, I always found her outside with her hose. She wanted me to stay too. "So many people retiring here now, nice people," she said. But I remembered how I had never gardened anything, not even a window box, and I left with the promise I'd come for another visit—when, I couldn't say.

In the Phoenix airport, the plane was late, not even taking off from Chicago yet, so I went to the Avis counter instead of the ticket counter. Do you see what I mean by an accident? But at that moment I just thought, a nice drive, a vacation that I deserved after all these years, and besides, by the time that plane gets here, I might already be with Rose, celebrating the first seder. "Tsuris, nothing but tsuris," Rose said, "asking for trouble," when I explained, but it turned out the drive was easy, all the way to the California border. Eight o'clock, a balmy spring night. Back in New York, it's still winter, freezing rain, snow maybe, certainly cold. And on the map California was skinny, so easy to drive across and come to Rose's while still she was watching the Tonight Show. When I noticed the gas getting low, I pulled out the map again to look at. The road looked short to Mecca and I could stretch my legs, get a cup of coffee, and visit the ladies' room.

But Mecca was further than I thought, and the road was very dark and narrow when the highway lights disappeared. I was scared but mostly of running out of gas and then the next day, where would I be? Stranded alone in the desert. "What mishegoss!" Rose said when I told her I ended up sleeping in the car's back seat, my skirt wrapped around my knees, but what else could I do, other than wait for morning? "Like a bag lady," she said but I hadn't thought of that. I was too busy trying not to be frightened. Before I fell asleep, I heard scurrying things outside but I knew they couldn't be

120

people, so I locked all the car doors and hoped for the best. In the morning, I fixed hair and lipstick in the rear-view mirror and headed on instead of back, which is what any sane person would have done—gone back to the main road. But I went on, looking for that gas station, because, God knows, it couldn't be far.

And you see, this is how I kissed an egret and how I ended up with Donna, but I'll get to that. The road ran between hills of sandy rock that had been made into craggy shapes—from too much scouring, I thought, like with a steel wool pad. There were a few dry squeaking trees, brown signs with no words, wheel tracks heading off into the canyons, and above a blue sky like its own river up there between the banks of the hills. I tried to tell Rose about the cool dry morning and how ahead of me were purple shadows made by strange shapes in the rocks and behind me was nothing but hot sun, but she said, "Oy, I don't understand this whole business of driving. You were supposed to fly. You know, the stewardesses tell jokes— funny ones even—while they show you how the seatbelt works." Then she said, "But you're here now," and we looked at each other, we who hadn't seen each other since Mama died, maybe a dozen years, a long long time. "You're here now," she repeated. "We're too old for such adventures. You're 70 years old, Rachel. My children are too old for such things now—sleeping in a car. Even the grandchildren have more sense; they at least bring a sleeping bag." Between talking, she wheezed. "It's not becoming," she said and stared at me just like she did when we were children and I did something wrong. Such a long time ago and the same look. She wanted me to stay, every day she told me. Her children wanted me to stay. I could take the other bedroom. The weather's so much better here, they said, and I would have things to do: there were concerts and museums, just like New York. And I could let in the night nurse, do the shopping and cooking, and call the doctors for appointments. I could pick the grandchildren up from school while Rose napped and wait for them at their piano lessons. "You're so good at taking care of things," Phyllis said. When Rose dozed off, I got up and looked out her window at the ocean and the palm trees and all the people in the park above the beach exchanging pictures of their grandchildren and playing canasta. I hadn't played since I don't know how long, but I remembered it used to be fun. If

I stayed, I'd have to learn again. We'd been down there earlier—me with a magazine and Rose with her oxygen canisters. Very pleasant—not too hot, the sun not too bright.

But I kept thinking about Mecca, a little nothing of a town laid out in the desert, where on Thursday morning every child in the county was coming for school—little ones dragging their backpacks on the dusty ground, teenage girls in short skirts, and boys driving fast in pick-up trucks. I drove around and around, avoiding those meshuggeneh teenage drivers and looking for some place to have breakfast, a cup of coffee at least, but there were no restaurants. Can you imagine—a town with no restaurants! Not even around the park, a little dried up square of brown grass where some dark men lounged in their big hats, and their dogs sat in the shade with their tongues hanging out of their mouths.

Finally on the edge of town, I found a store, clean at least, attached to the gas station. Inside, like a deli—back home we'd call it a deli—but here there were cookies, frosted pink and with a look like packed sand, and a glass case full of some type of sandwich wrapped in bright yellow paper where there should have been bagels and cream cheese. I bought a cup of coffee and a big cookie with sprinkles and pointed to one of the sandwiches in the case. "Burrito?" the girl behind the counter asked and I got through the rest of the transaction with sign language, lots of nodding, and a *gracias*, though I was worried—was I pronouncing it properly? I tried to remember what Spanish I'd learned on the streets of New York but every phrase made me blush. When I handed over my money, she said "Thank you" in perfect English. What had I been thinking? California, I needed to keep reminding myself, not Mexico! Now I laugh at my foolishness. I walked around the town, what there was of it. Like a tourist! When I had seen the stucco houses, the gas station, and the little drugstore—a "pharmacia," then I stood by the school fence, eating my "burrito" and watching all the little ones getting off the buses, because where else could I go in that poor ugly town? What would those men have said—very nice men, I'm sure—about an older Jewish lady sitting down under their tree with them to eat? No, I couldn't do that. "Oy, Rachel, such chozzerai," Rose said when I told her about my breakfast. "A burrito is full of lard. Terrible for the heart, my Danny says." But, I said, the coffee tasted of cinnamon. Maybe they would have talked to me, would have let me rub the dogs' bellies with a stick.

Later in the day, again Rose started in, between complaining about the wait at her doctor's and about the friends who would be coming for cards. "You'll be staying," she said again, like an order more than a question. "I don't need much. Just someone here to make sure I don't stop breathing. I'll just stay in my room, and the whole apartment will be yours."

I said, "I'm here, Rosie. Don't worry."

"And why, Rachel, why did you keep driving? Why didn't you stop earlier? Why not stay in a motel a second night, you can afford this, no? Still I don't understand."

"What's to understand?" I said. "I thought I would be here faster," but she waved her hand at me as if something smelled bad, because already she understood, before I did even, that I would be leaving.

In Mecca I stared at the dingy Chamber of Commerce sign: "Eastern Gateway to the Salton Sea," it read. "Largest Body of Water in California." And I picked up a brochure. The lake was formed, it said, in 1905 when an irrigation canal failed. The flooding lasted sixteen months, until boxcars filled with rocks were used to dam the flow. Sixteen months of water flowing into a valley that used to be underwater. It was flowing back toward its home. Largest body of water? The lake was forty-five miles long and twenty-five miles wide, but I'd never heard of it. Rose never said.

At the gas station, I asked the quickest way to Route 10 and Los Angeles, and the man pointed me north, not back the way I came. "Are you sure?" I asked.

"Si, up through Indio. Takes you right there."

And there, another little mistake, following his advice— shorter maybe but the road took me so that I could glimpse this Salton Sea. Maybe my sister was right—what normal person would drive around in the heat, in the desert, already the asphalt shimmering, prickly things and gray bushes piled up against fences. I drove alongside a railway track on which freight cars rumbled. Then the road turned right, and there it was, a pale blue lake so long I couldn't see its southern end, a mechiaeh—like a turquoise in a ring. Really, it was that pretty, and I skipped my turn-off. Again crazy instead of sane. The road drove through green fields of something growing but I didn't know what, then desert again, then oranges and palm trees. When I told Rose I'd seen orange groves, she said, "Oranges I can get you here, as big as your head nearly, nothing like those hard green balls we got in Brooklyn as kids. And remember how Mama always made us eat them with a glass of milk. The acid wasn't good for our stomachs, she said. Well I've learned since then, it's just not so. For once, Mama was wrong."

When I told her I'd walked through groves of date palms, she sighed again. "Palms, shmalms," she said. "There are palms here," and she lifted her hand above her head. We were outside as usual in the early morning, in the park, and there were palm trees all around, sprinkling us with their shade. "And dates, here I can buy you dates all the way from Arabia, you want dates." She tapped my knee.

I said, "You'd like it, Rosie, so much to look at. Maybe we could go back there for a visit. You know, just like Israel, they turn the desert into a garden. Then there's a fence, the water stops, and boom—desert again. So strange..."

"Yes, irrigation. I know about irrigation, Rachel."

"And it's so bright....," I said but then I remembered—her conversion. My sister had raised her children by the backyard pool, but since her best friend got skin cancer fifteen years ago, she has not left the house between ten in the morning and four in the afternoon. Similar to her conversion from Reform to Conservative that happened when David, her husband, died.

She said, "So what do you need with that? You know how terrible sun is for the skin. And you especially, someone who spent her whole life indoors. Besides," she said, "there's plenty light here, just open the curtains. And here, it's so close to the hospital, just in case—God forbid—anything should happen. And what would you do there? Here, there's the library for books, and a synagogue. Here you can hear the symphony at the Hollywood Bowl. I can't go—the walk from the bus, it's all up hill, and besides, the seats there are so hard, three cushions you need to shlep. But you, Rachel, you're younger...." I didn't understand why with each sentence I felt older not younger, until, finally, I felt my age. The fog came in off the ocean and I felt the arthritis in my fingers. The sun went down and I couldn't see. I woke in the middle of the night and couldn't sleep, so hobbled around the apartment,

124

afraid I would trip, fall, break a hip. I kept thinking, the life here is better than Mama's in New York where she couldn't go outside all winter because of the ice. But when Phyllis came the next morning, my favorite niece, I didn't want to talk to her. At breakfast, I complained the orange juice was pulpy, the lox cut too thick, and the coffee was too strong. Already, I too was a kvetch.

And then at the sign for Salton City, I turned off the main road. I kept driving because once I saw the water, I wanted to get closer. "Water," I thought, "lunch. I might as well." Streets ran off, with a neat sign at each corner: Paradise Lane, Oleander Drive. And there really were pink flowering bushes—oleanders?—growing, and down one street, a tank truck even, watering them, but hardly any houses anywhere. The streets were waiting for them to be built. Closer to the water, there were some houses—just one here, one there, along all those streets—all the blinds drawn, some cactus in the yard, and a boat pulled up to the top of the driveway.

And the man I met at the dock, in his greasy garage coveralls, kinky hair gone gray, skin a nice mahogany color but dusty—Rose would think that was crazy too, just talking to him. And why did I anyway? Rose would have tossed her head the way she did in high school when a boy she didn't like came to speak with her: she'd toss and walk away. And from riding the subway all these years I have made my own way to fend off strangers: I clutch my handbag to my stomach and look right through them. But this time I didn't. I saw him fishing, then I went and stood behind him. In a white plastic bucket, I could hear something thumping. Finally he said, "Pretty lucky today," without turning around, and I crouched down and watched him fish. It was hot, dry like an oven, so I fanned myself with a map from my purse to make a little breeze and watched the little blue waves lapping all along the treeless shore and the sun move around and hit the mountains, brown like corrugated boxes, on the eastern side of the lake, pretty even, so long as you didn't breathe through the nose—it didn't smell very nice. When I could feel the perspiration run down my chest and my stockings stick to my legs, I stood to walk away.

"Don't go yet. Dontcha want to see me catch something?" he chuckled, and goodness knows why, I stayed to see, though

125

my head kept telling me, "Rosie will be worrying about you. Already it will be dark by the time you reach her." But maybe I got sunstroke or some other sickness out there. Or maybe the ugly smell from the lake was some sort of a drug because I stayed and stayed. Finally he reeled one in, a gray and scaly fish, the size of his two dark hands. He unhooked it and held it out to me, still flopping and flapping. "Whoa," he said, and grabbed it tighter. "That's Tilapia. That's some good eating. Pretty much the only fish that'll stay alive in here." He waved it at me, smiling. "Take it. Take it," he said, "come on now. But don't kill it till you get home." When he saw me shrinking back, he laughed, put it in a plastic bag with some water. "Now come on, take it," he said and laughed some more and patted me on the arm with a slimy, fishy hand, until I had to take it, just to make him stop. What do you do with a live fish when you don't have a knife to kill it or a kitchen or even a bucket to keep it alive in? I thought of slipping it back into the lake. To tell the truth, the whole place smelled fetid, like sulfur and salt. I could see there were dead fish floating near the shore. But I didn't want to hurt his feelings either. I was embarrassed to think of him watching me put his catch back in the water, so I just thanked him and started to walk away.

126

"If you're not from around here, you can take that to Johnson's Landing and Donna'll cook it up for you," he called after me. "It's just about the only restaurant around, just around that bend."

Well, OK, I thought, it was past lunch time anyway. "Now you're eating poisoned fish!" my sister said when I told her. "And when there's a new deli here that, I swear, makes kreplach like you haven't tasted since Mama died."

My mouth began to water. Mama would spend a whole day in the kitchen and come out dusted with flour. To the table, she would bring the bowls of chicken soup and kreplach, chewy dough filled with ground meat, onions, chicken fat. On special occasions—on Purim or to break the fast on Yom Kippur—she drew hopeful messages, Hebrew letters, into the dough so that Rose and I and our brother Itzhak would swallow God's blessings. "She's in a better place," I said, remembering her last years in the nursing home that you had to check every day were they bathing her and changing her clothes when she soiled them. She lived to 95, but she could still recognize me thank goodness, at least enough to know I was the one to complain to. Rose visited once every year, the same time she came to visit Papa's grave. I always got to the home early that day, made sure Mama was clean and dressed in her best, wearing the latest piece of jewelry Rose had sent that otherwise I kept at home, or her roommate, an even older lady but cunning, would steal it.

I stumbled along the shore, wishing I'd changed into some other shoes, until I saw it—a white shack on salt-crusted pilings out over the water with a big red sign and flowering cactuses all along the front. Inside the air conditioning was on and it was cool and dark. There were some canned goods on shelves, a soda machine, a bar, two covered pool tables with, in the middle of each, a vase of flowers. A young woman bent over the counter, her long dark hair falling and covering her face. She was reading a magazine, and when she looked up, I saw she was Japanese. Maybe I was in the wrong place. In the background, I heard a television going. Then I realized I was holding the fish in its bag in front of me like something dirty. "Oy, how silly," I said, waving the bag. "Are you Donna?" I asked, unsure.

"Who else?" She smiled at me. "Did Vick give that to you from the lake? Ugly, isn't it? I don't eat those—I hear the water's full of chemicals from all the farming round here. Do you want it for your lunch?"

"Oh no, thank you. I don't think so," I said.

"Well, here, give it to me." She held out her hand for the bag. "I'll have the kids take it back to the lake when their show's over. I can't drag them away from it. They're home sick from school today. I'll put it in the sink for now." Then she came back with her order pad, and I noticed she was looking me up and down, leaning over the counter, even, to see my bottom half—my skirt all wrinkled from sleeping, my heels all coated with mud. "You're not from around here, are you?" and before I could answer, she asked, "You're not lost?"

"Oh no, I have a map," I said. "I'm going to visit my sister in Santa Monica, but I got off the highway to... well, it's too long a story. Now I see I might as well head to San Diego and then drive north. I need to start again soon."

"Well, San Diego's pretty nice. Least that's what the kids tell me. Their Dad lives there."

"Oh," I said and looked down at her order pad. Her hand was still poised to write. Her fingernails were painted pale

127

pink, the color of carnations. "I'll have a turkey sandwich." I watched her paint mayonnaise onto the bread slices. I'd never seen someone make a sandwich so slowly. It would take forever and when would I get back on the road? "My, I'm hungry," I said, but she didn't fix the sandwich any more quickly. "Well, it's nice and cool in here, anyway, isn't it?"

"Deadly out there. I keep the lights low too. That helps."

When she brought the sandwich over, she had a sad look and she kept looking at me as I started to eat. "I'm sorry," I said.

"Sorry?"

"About your husband," I said.

"My ex? He's OK. He sends money when he can. And he's good to the girls, takes them for a couple weeks every summer, takes them to Disneyland at Christmas too. He's a trucker so even if we were still together, they'd hardly see him. It just didn't work out with us is all. He never even yelled that I can remember."

She took it all so smoothly. "Oh," was all I could think to say.

"Maybe that was it," she said, thoughtfully. "Someone not yelling can be terrible, can't it?"

We laughed together and I ate the sandwich. Soon her children, two girls, came into the dining room and climbed up onto stools at the end of the counter. Both with her mouth and eyes, but with freckles too and brown hair done up in braids that looked as though they'd been slept on. They didn't look a bit sick.

"What have you been watching?" I asked.

"*Mole People*," the one closer to me said, the littler one. "It's really neat. There're these people who live underground. They're all white and these other guys find them, sort of by mistake, I think. They're evil—the mole people, I mean—but the other guys get them with this big flashlight."

When she paused for breath, her mother said, "I think that's enough, Sue. We barely know what you're talking about."

"But Mom, she asked."

"Why don't you do something for me? Get out of the house for a few minutes and take this fish back to the lake, will you?"

"Aw, it's so hot out there," the older girl complained, but she slid off her stool and pulled her sister after her. They took the fish in its plastic bag but they lingered, kicking the screen door open and letting it slam shut. Their mother went over, put her hands on their shoulders. "Hey, you're letting all the hot air in." She gave them a little shove out the door. "You can have ice cream when you come back," she called after them.

"What nice girls," I said.

She wiped her hands on a towel. "Sometimes I just let them stay home," she said. "They keep me from talking to the radio. It's not too busy round here, you can see. Sometimes I get a crowd on the weekend when the fishing's good and sometimes a couple people want to stick around late playing pool but otherwise..." She'd been there for over ten years, she said, first with her husband and now alone. Still, she wasn't really thinking of leaving. "Some fools—me included—thought this could be a second Palm Springs! You know, lots of rich white people on vacation, spending money!"

"But it's so quiet here," I said. "Wouldn't people come just for that?"

"You've got to be kidding," she said and laughed. "It's hot. It's smelly. And it's miles from nowhere. My parents won't even come visit from LA. They say the desert reminds them of the camps."

"The camps?" The word is a curse, involuntary cringing. Suddenly the room was very cold.

"You know. They were in Oklahoma during the war," she said, "before I was born."

When the girls came back in, they got up on the stools again, waved their hands wildly in front of their faces. "It's hot out there, Mom. Where's that ice cream?" the older one said.

The younger one came over and stood in front of me silently, rubbing her damp hair out of her face. "Do you know how to make braids?" she asked. "These are a mess."

"Leave the lady alone now," Donna said, "she needs to leave soon," but the girl didn't move. She just stood in front of me, tugging on the ends of her braids.

"Of course I know how to make braids," I said. I held my arms out to her and she turned around and stood between my knees. While I struggled with the tangles, Donna turned the radio on to a country station. When the song changed, she grabbed her daughters. "This is it," she said, "the song I've been telling you about. Come on Sue, Misha, I'll teach you that dance." They stomped and kicked and twirled across the floor, the girls giggling every time they got the steps wrong, their mother yelling, "That's it, that's it," every time they got it right.

I sat uncomfortable on my stool at the counter, watching them dance, waiting to pay my check. "I never had children," I thought suddenly and it was as if someone pulled a plug and tears came to my eyes. "Of course, you didn't," I thought. "How could you with no husband? And working all the time. And besides, there were Itzhak's kids, those three beautiful babies who ended up with no father. And then later Rose's kids came east for school and stayed with you summer vacations while they worked in the city. Remember how you liked to take Phyllis shopping for her winter college clothes at Gimble's and how you liked it when Danny took you out to dinner, just the two of you like a Mother and son on a date. And now, all the grandnieces and grandnephews," I thought and started to list their names in my head. The tears disappeared again, and by the time the song was over, I was fine, just fine. "Let me finish those braids," I said. And when a waltz came on the radio, I said, "Would you like me to teach you?" and Sue nodded her head vigorously, and I was happy to show her and her sister the fundamentals of the waltz. Rose and I had often practiced the waltz and the fox trot together, and the tango too when Mama wasn't looking. We dreamed of reincarnation as the dancing Levine sisters.

When the news came on, Donna turned the radio off. "Well, you girls need to call up and find out what your homework is. I'm not letting you stay home another day," she said. "And I've got to get to those books. It's almost tax time and it always takes me forever cause I never really know what I'm doing, even after all these years."

"And I need to go to my sister," I said.

Donna walked me to the door. Outside, the sun had gone down. Can you believe it? I'd spent that much time without even noticing. The sky in the west was turning pink. To the east, the lake and the Chocolate Mountains behind it were all one creamy brown-pink smear, like a Necco wafer. When I pulled the car keys from my purse, Donna said, "It'll be getting dark soon, you know. You don't really want to be driving all that way in the dark, do you?"

130

And that was that. That's how I came to stay with her. One night, I thought, but then I started to help with her taxes and stayed three days. After helping Mr. Jenson with his books twenty years, the skills came in helpful, helpful to someone who really needed some help. When we put the finished forms in the mail, Donna gave me a big hug. I shrank back, but she said, "You don't know what a relief that is. Now, tell me what I can do for you."

"Where have you been?" my sister insisted when I finally arrived at her apartment Monday noon. "We've been waiting and waiting."

"Ah, our missing person," Danny joked when he came from the kitchen holding a glass of something dark over ice.

"We even called the police we were so worried," my niece said, "but they wouldn't start looking for another day."

I reminded them I'd called—I did call and say I would be delayed. I explained it was an accident, a series of little accidents all piling up, and everything else—really, how I myself didn't know how it had taken me so long to reach her, but Rose sighed with exasperation. "Like a crazy child," she said. "Just like you always were Rachel," she said. "You remember Aunt Mildred? how she used to go to the store in her slippers and come back with only a box of cookies, not even Kosher? And now you spent half of Pesach in the desert…. Listen, Rachel, you stay here and Danny will help." 131

I remembered we laughed at Mildred but now I think maybe that was all she wanted, a box of Mallomars.

Rose's voice was the same as I remembered, coarser but still reedy like an oboe is reedy, musical that is. And my head, as I stood in her living room, it was still full of the sound of the typewriter bell when it hit the end of the carriage and the buzzing of the computer when it saved a file. It was full of sirens and subway trains and the garbled voices that come over the loudspeakers in the subway stations, especially Union Square. *Beware of the moving platform….* I could still hear the voices of all my nieces and nephews too, at all different ages— the babies when they clamored for something sweet, the older ones with their stories of parties and classes. And Mr. Jenson wishing me good morning and then his friendly bellow: "Oh Rachel, oh Rachel, you're needed here." So many noises inside my skull. Why wouldn't they go away?

I have only one thing left to tell you really, and that is how I kissed the egret. Sunday, Donna took us for a drive. "Come on," she said, "Margolita's here to watch the place. Let me show you around." We got in her car and drove south, past green growing fields and orange and grapefruit groves with the fruit shining between the leaves like Christmas decorations, the girls in the back seat.

Desert passed by with little dry bushes growing in sand. Then when water glistened in ditches, there were brilliant green fields... "That's alfalfa, I think," Donna said. Then another field.

"That's onions!" I said.

"More onions!" Sue and Misha cried.

I saw row after row of green onion stalks, and in the dirt I could see the white onions, almost like eggs or bones. The car filled with the smell of onions, as if you had just cut one in half to grate for latkes. "This soil must be very good," I said, looking at all the growing things.

"Only because they irrigate," Donna said. "Only because of all that stuff they pour into it, fertilizers and I don't know what else."

"And all the water's stolen from the Colorado River," Misha added. "It used to run into the Gulf and it's not supposed to be here at all. They built about six dams though. Now it's just a swamp where the river used to go."

When the road curved, we drove through a town that was nothing but shacks, tin warehouses, garages, fertilizer stores, and one dusty motel—even uglier than Mecca, even less than Salton City. Then we turned again and headed to the lake, now from the south. In the distance, there were some buildings with concrete domes, clouds of white steam coming from them. "What are those?" I asked.

"Geothermal plants," Donna said. "The Magma Energy Company—isn't that a goofy name? The kids got to go there for a field trip but I had to stay with the store. Misha, you explained it to me. How does it work again?"

"There's hot water, really hot, deep down in the ground, and they.... Do you really want to hear about this?"

"Yes." I turned around to see her. "Tell me how it works."

"They pump the hot water up, and when it hits the air, it turns into steam, and the steam turns the turbines. All the heat gets turned into electricity—somehow. I don't remember that part so well. People used to think it was a really clean way to get energy but it makes air pollution too. And noise. And when they put the cold water back into the ground, it can make earthquakes happen."

We kept driving and I realized I was in a very strange place, where things did not go together in the way I was used to, ugly and pretty at the same time, where Japanese mothers danced some country music jig, where you needed a shmatte bobby-pinned on to keep the hot wind from blowing your hair, where you brought the smell of living vegetables and dead, salty fish into the house with you every time. "Where are you taking me?" I asked.

"Just around. You'll see," was all Donna said.

"I know where," Sue said. "It's a surprise."

We were driving on smaller and smaller roads until we pulled up at a bird sanctuary. "This is one of my favorite places," Donna said. We walked along a marsh—Donna lent me gym shoes this time—scaring rabbits, lizards and roadrunners out of the underbrush, then the grasses split and there was the lake. White pelicans swooped overhead and avocets dipped with the black and white stripes along their backs and grebes swam and sandpipers poked along in the mud. I looked them all up busily in a pamphlet I'd picked up. The girls ran around in circles. At the foot of a hill, we saw a burrowing owl sitting calmly on a post. It eyed us but didn't move until I pulled my camera out—already I wanted a photo to prove to Rose there was more here than dust. Then we all sat on a bench near the water, and a cool breeze blew. It seemed thousands of ducks were floating on the lake—a convention, a conference, all headed in the same direction. Even the girls were quiet. Then out of the sky, a great white bird came sweeping, wings spread wide wide wide. It landed near us on long skinny legs and ruffled the long plumes on its back and we sat so still it didn't fly away. Sue held my arm tight. Donna leaned close. "An egret," she whispered in my ear. Slowly, I held out my hand—I don't know why. My hand was empty, no fish to entice it, but the bird came closer, until it looked right up at my face with that quick pecking birdie look that even sparrows in Central Park have. It looked at me like my nieces and nephews used to look at me when I baby-sat, when they wanted something and neither of us could figure

133

out what it was. I moved my hand but the egret stayed. I remember Mama wanting a hat with egret plumes, a blue hat so it looked like a bird on water, but she could never afford it. And I learned later almost all these birds died to make such hats. I touched the bird's neck, its crest, but it didn't startle. It actually stepped closer and tipped its beak up. If it had opened its mouth and spoken, I wouldn't have been surprised, but it didn't. It just stood there, so I bent down and kissed it, kissed the spot right above the beak. The feathers were soft—of course they were—and I smelled fish and salt and a completely new smell that must be the smell of live birds. I heard Donna gasp and the girls gasp, so I gasped too—what <u>was</u> I doing? "Feh!" Rose would say, "dirty." And then the egret hopped back and flew off, disappearing into a great flock of other egrets wheeling above, as if it had never been there in front of us.

Monday noon I arrived in Santa Monica, and six days later, I called the family together in Rose's living room. "I've decided," I said. "I'll come visit, but I won't stay. This time, I am the one to leave." My voice was shaking and I needed to sit down in the middle of my speech.

"All these years...," she said. "So you were upset that I left. Who would know? But Rachel, you were the baby, you were always the favorite, that's why I left."

Her children were silent. They looked at their hands.

"Me, the favorite?"

"Yes, it was true. Mama always made a dish special for you. Papa gave you books. Me, he gave something little he didn't care about, a hair clip, a sewing kit. Ah, enough of that. This place you've found, I don't understand, but if you like it.... And you know you're always welcome here."

On the dock, I sit, just sit, happy to be back. Happy? What is that? I don't know that. The lake is blue and the waves make little lapping sounds—otherwise silence. As usual the water smells bad. The dead fish float but maybe not so many as last week. I sit on the dock anyway, where Vick baits hooks and spills gasoline for his boat, where birds have relieved themselves. Just a few days ago, I came here in my nylons and could barely think to crouch. Now I have an old black cotton skirt, the one I used to wear only for house cleaning, and no shoes and sitting right on this smelly dock. Up above, the sky is pale yellowish blue like always just after sunset, and the Chocolate Mountains fade pink into the lake. Overhead there are the silver glints of Navy jets. ("Don't go driving off onto the bomb range, now," Donna told me when I was heading for Indio to get us some groceries.) I wish I could say it was all very nice but this place isn't like that, not right off. It will take a long time for all the noises in my head to go quiet, all the people talking to me and all the machines I've heard clanging and banging and whining and whistling, all the radio programs and television programs; it will take many days of reading, walking, and continuing the dancing lessons with Sue and Misha. The sky turns orange, then pink, then violet, and the colors reflect in the lake's waters like flowers, like double flowers. I am like them—an accident, a switch being turned in the brain by mistake, water pushing through a levee, like a medication that pushes the cells apart, like blooming. On the way back from seeing the egret we stopped at a date grove, and seventy feet up, I saw a man working, with his hands buried in a cluster of bright yellow flowers. "He's pollinating," Donna said. He tied the male flowers into the female and placed a net bag over all, no good relying on wind to do the job. I thought, the man's hands must get filthy, coated with golden pollen.

135

Suddenly Daniel, I think: Daniel. I have never told anyone about Daniel, our decade-long Thursday afternoons affair, Daniel with the limp that kept him from the war, but he made me open, like the brightness here—everything tight loosening up. My legs spread wider and wider, my hands grasped the headboard. Why would I remember that now? I'm afraid even Donna might find it sordid, the hotel room with a window opening on the airshaft, my dream that never happened of one time spending a whole night with him in one of the big rooms overlooking Gramercy Park. Sometimes it would be his child's birthday and he would come with a present, a big box wrapped up in paper. He'd try to hide it from me, to spare my feelings, and that made me almost cry, almost as nice as if the present were for me (though what would I have needed with a doll or a toy railroad, I don't know). Still, once we were undressed, once we were in bed.... And now forty years without it, my goodness forty years! The other day, when Donna touched my wrist—that's the feeling I had. Oh, not as strong of course, not really the same of course, but still it was skin on skin. Ah, all that was years, no, decades ago, and now Daniel is gone with the others—Itzhak; our parents; Itzhak's daughter to leukemia; my best friend from high school, Leah, who died trying to get rid of a baby; Rose's husband David; and Rose soon too. She sounds sharp to me but Phyllis says how difficult it is for her to breathe (how could she have stopped sunning but not smoking!). "No use crying," Papa always said and snapped his *New York Times* out full width to read. But some things are worth crying over, I think and I remember his bald head, all freckled. I see a silver glint high up, another jet. Here, they practice bombing things, they suck energy up from the ground and let chemicals seep down into it and into the water so things can grow, they pay people nothing nearly to pick those fruits which is terrible, but still, there is a space to breathe. It's almost dark now, just an orange glow up there, up above. A few tears, and then suddenly, absurd, I realize I'm filled with some feeling I don't know. Each cell pulses, moving fast with freedom. I can't imagine how they stay together in this one body. The world tastes sweet and there's so little time. Breathless, I think, stunned, "This is joy!"

136

Notes

Grateful acknowledgement is made to the University of Washington Graduate School Fund, the Oregon State University Center for the Humanities, and the Oregon State University College of Liberal Arts for their generous support of this project.

Many thanks to the following people for their encouragement, thoughtful advice, and faith in these stories: Tracy Daugherty, Cheryl Glenn, Ann Mine, Claire Needell, Rick Peabody, David Shields, Linda Zerilli, and especially my husband, John Robinson.

To the following—thanks for the inspiration: Atget; Baudelaire's *Paris Spleen, 1869*; *The Cabinet of Dr. Caligari*; Julio Cortazar; Jacques-Louis David; Rainer Werner Fassbinder; Freud's *Mourning and Melancholia*; Hal Hartley; Billie Holiday; Chris Isaak; Henry James; Kristeva's *Black Sun: Depression and Melancholia*; kd lang; the Museum of Jurassic Technology; Nirvana; Roy Orbison; the Plimsouls; Douglas Sirk; Wim Wenders; Virginia Woolf; Yo La Tengo.

A number of these stories required more specific research, and I am indebted to the following books and authors:
  for "Throwing Voices," William Labov's *Language in the Inner City: Studies in the Black English Vernacular*
  for "Memento Mori," Susan Stewart's *On Longing*; Chris Bonnington's *The Everest Years: a Climber's Life and Quest for Adventure*; and especially Jon Krakauer's *Into the Wild* and *Eiger Dreams: Ventures among Men and Mountains*
  for "Noctambus," Greil Marcus's *Ranters & Crowd Pleasers: Punk in Pop Music 1977-92*, especially "Life After Death"
  for "Proximity to the Body of the Star," *The Adoring Audience*, edited by Lisa A. Lewis; *Stardom: Industry of Desire*, edited by Christine Gledhill; *Claims to Fame: Celebrity in Contemporary America* by Joshua Gamson; *Marilyn Monroe* by Maurice Zolotow; and *Dead Elvis: a Chronicle of a Cultural Obsession* by Greil Marcus

Printed in the United States
73168LV00002B/184-231